They both heard someone ringing a hand bell as a signal that they were to return to the barge. Harriet made to leave, but he held her back. He turned her to him and looked down at her, at that passionate mouth.

"No," she said faintly, but he bent his head and covered her mouth with his own.

The feelings she experienced were devastating. She found she could not hold back and returned his kiss with her whole heart. At last he held her tight and leaned his cheek against hers, feeling her body tremble against his own. The bell sounded once more. He took her arm again. "We do not want to be left behind," he said.

By Marion Chesney
Published by Fawcett Books:

THE CHOCOLATE DEBUTANTE

Marion Chesney

FAWCETT CREST • NEW YORK

A Fawcett Crest Book
Published by Ballantine Books
Copyright © 1995 by Marion Chesney

Library of Congress Catalog Card Number: 95-90419

ISBN 0-449-22259-4

Manufactured in the United States of America

First Edition: October 1995

10 9 8 7 6 5 4 3 2 1

Chapter One

MISS HARRIET TREMAYNE read the letter from her sister several times as if wishing to read something else altogether in it than what was there. The fact that her sister, Mrs. Colville, said she was dangerously ill did not distress Harriet. Mary Colville was always ill with some imaginary illness or another. What did upset her was that her sister was begging her to bring her daughter, Susan, out at the forthcoming Season.

To refuse, as the reclusive and intellectual Harriet longed to do, would mean that the whole Colville family would arrive at her town house in Berkeley Square and she would have them *all* for the Season instead of just one debutante. Mrs. Colville had six children, Susan being the eldest. Harriet frowned. She had not seen Susan for some years, for the girl had been secluded in an expensive seminary for young ladies in Bath, but she remembered her as a fat and rather pimply child.

After some hard thought she decided the best course of action would be to travel to her sister, who lived in the village of Parton-in-the-Wold, and decide when she saw Susan what to do. Should the girl prove an absolute antidote, then she would plead the excuse of foreign travel, tell the Colville family that they might have the use of her house for the Season, and then go into hiding until it was all over.

Harriet was rich, very rich. A magnificent legacy from an aunt who admired intellectual bluestockings like Harriet had saved her from having to go on the marriage market and find a husband. She knew she was damned as eccentric, but she was content with the company of her few female friends and had never pined for balls and parties. But she was well connected and knew that she could drum up the necessary invitations to launch Susan on a successful Season.

So she began to make preparations to leave for the country, wishing all the same that the weather might improve, for the month of January was bitterly cold and the Thames had been frozen so long that a Frost Fair was being held on it with booths and amusements from one shore of the river to the other.

She had her own traveling carriage and coachman and so did not have to endure the rigors of the mail coach or the stage. She set out three days later, sensibly dressed, for she had never troubled about being fashionable. She was wearing a dark blue wool gown, a fur-lined cloak, serviceable boots, and a serviceable bonnet. She knew she would need to spend two days on the road, but was armed with a collection of books. There were hot bricks on the floor of the well-sprung carriage and she planned to spend the first night at an expensive and well-run posting inn.

She traveled in some style. She had her maid, Lucy, with her inside, a groom on the roof with the coachman, armed with a blunderbuss, two footmen

2

on the back strap, and two outriders, armed to the teeth.

Lucy was a quiet, middle-aged woman of grim visage and not much conversation. Harriet had employed her because of her silence rather than because of any talents she might have had as a lady's maid, and would have been surprised had she known that the quiet maid longed to see her mistress dressed in the latest fashions. But there had never been any man in Harriet's rich, well-ordered life to spur her on to "prettify" herself. She was a woman of middle height with thick jet black hair, large green eyes, and a thin, clever face.

Nothing exciting had ever happened to Harriet, and she dreamed of neither romance nor adventure. The immense relief she had felt when she had learned about her legacy had never left her, and she felt she was the most fortunate of women. Most of the friends of her youth produced baby after baby with clockwork regularity and were worn out by the time they had reached her age. Some were married to brutish men and some to fools. Her gratitude for her single state kept her tranquil and happy.

The sky outside the carriage windows was dark and leaden. She asked the maid to light the lamp inside the carriage so that she might see to read, and settled back to her book. Lucy did as she was bid and then sat down again opposite her mistress.

She had been employed as maid by Harriet shortly after the death of Harriet's parents. The late Mr. Tremayne had been a feckless gambler and had left little but debts. Then the week after the funeral the news of her legacy had arrived. Lucy remembered how she had assumed that after a

3

period of mourning, the young Harriet would find a suitable lady to sponsor her at the Season. She had been amazed when Harriet, only twenty, had announced her determination to sell the family home and estates in the country and move to London to set up her own residence. For once the usually silent Lucy had found her voice to suggest that Miss Tremayne find a chaperone. But Harriet had merely looked amused and said she had been given a passport to freedom from marriage and childbearing.

The friends that Harriet had made in London, Lucy found boring. They were sensible, plain-featured, bookish ladies, much given to debating on subjects Lucy thought ought to be left to the men. The only social events Harriet attended were the playhouse and the opera. At the opera she did not visit anyone in the other boxes, and no one visited her, and she never went to the opera ball. At the playhouse she arrived at the beginning of the play and left at the end before the harlequinade.

There had been various suitors attracted by her fortune, but Harriet had managed to snub them all.

Lucy knew of the reason for this journey and hoped Harriet would sponsor her niece. The maid settled back comfortably, placed her feet on one of the hot bricks, and dreamed of showing off her handiwork to society. She did hope the girl would turn out to be pretty.

Harriet stopped for the night at the Cromwell Posting House at four in the afternoon. What light there had been during the day was fast fading from the sky, and snowflakes were beginning to whirl about the carriage as it drove under the game-festooned arch of the posting house. In the entrance hall, sides of beef and pies were exhibited in glass cases like precious objets d'art. The landlord came out, bowing and scraping. Harriet had stopped at his posting house before on her infrequent visits to her sister. She was conducted upstairs to a handsome bedchamber and told that her usual private parlor had been reserved for her. Dinner would be served at five.

Harriet washed and changed. Lucy, who had been feeling travel sick for the last stage of the journey, asked if she might have a tray in her room. Harriet agreed, saw that the inn servants had been instructed to look after her maid's comfort, made sure the other servants were comfortably housed, took a worried look out at the fast-falling snow, and then went to the private parlor at the end of the corridor, prepared to enjoy her dinner, for the posting house had a good cook and she found she was extremely hungry.

She stopped short on the threshold. A man was standing by the fireplace with one booted foot resting on the fender. He was extremely tall and powerfully built. As if conscious of her stare, he swung around and surveyed her. He had very red hair, which he wore unpowdered, a handsome face if somewhat harsh gray eyes, a proud nose, firm mouth, and long eyelashes that did not detract from the masculinity of his face but paradoxically seemed to highlight it.

He raised thin eyebrows and said haughtily, "Madam?"

Harriet bowed her head rather than dropping a curtsy. "Sir, you are in my private parlor."

"I must correct you. I hired it." He turned back to the fire as if the matter were settled. Whoever this man was, he expected lesser mortals to give way to his demands.

"Waiter!" shouted Harriet. When a waiter came hurrying along the corridor, she said, "Fetch the landlord. This is *my* parlor for *my* use and I wish this gentleman ejected from it as soon as possible. I shall await the landlord in my room." And with that, Harriet stalked off.

A few moments later the landlord scratched at the door and she went to open it. "Miss Tremayne," he said, "there has been a dreadful mistake. I was ill with the French cold"—he meant influenza, the French being blamed for most ills—"and my wife took the Earl of Dangerfield's booking."

"Then you will just need to unbook Lord Dangerfield," said Harriet waspishly.

"But he is an earl and . . ."

"Do you expect me to dine in the common dining room?"

"There are very few customers because of the weather, and such that we have are most genteel," pleaded the landlord. "I could put a screen about your table."

"Oh, very well," said Harriet. "But I will not stay at this posting house again."

The miserable landlord went into the private parlor. "Who was that female?" demanded the earl.

"A Miss Tremayne, my lord. Do not worry, Miss Tremayne has agreed to take her food in the dining room."

"But you have other private parlors!"

"The roof was leaking so one is being painted, and the sweep is to clean the chimney in the other tomorrow, so everything there is sheeted."

6

The earl frowned. "I will eat in the dining room. Tell Miss Tremayne she may have the parlor."

"Thank you, my lord. It will be very quiet, most of the other guests having dined at four."

The landlord made his way toward the dining room, followed by the earl.

But when they entered the dining room, Harriet was seated at a table by the fire and already drinking soup. She listened with raised brows as the landlord explained that the earl had most graciously given up the private parlor.

"I wish he had done so in the first place," said Harriet tartly. "As you can see, I have already begun to dine. Let him have it."

The handsome earl, who was used to having females practically throw themselves at his feet, studied Miss Harriet Tremayne, and she looked straight back at him.

"The fire is pleasant here. I will join Miss Tremayne for dinner," he said. The landlord rushed off to find the waiter.

"This is too much," said Harriet evenly as he sat down opposite her. "There are other tables." She was at the only small table. The others were large and round, catering as they did to large parties or mail-coach passengers. Stagecoaches were not welcome at the posting house. "You are forcing your company on me."

Lord Dangerfield could not quite believe that his company was not welcome.

At that moment the door of the dining room opened and a party of bloods came in. They were the worse for drink, noisy, and staring about them.

Harriet had the grace to smile. "It looks as if I

7

may need the protection of your company after all, my lord."

He was piqued by her indifference to him, he had to admit that, but his sense of humor came to his rescue, and he smiled back at her.

The men were seating themselves at a large table at the window. One stumbled and swore. The earl got to his feet and walked over to them. "There is a lady present," he said, "and if any of you uses language like that again, I will have to call you out."

The five men stared at him, and then one said, "It's Dangerfield, isn't it? I'm Tommy Burke. Saw you at Tat's the other day, buying a prime piece of blood."

"Then, Mr. Burke, perhaps you would be so good as to muzzle your companions?"

"No offense meant, Dangerfield, and none taken, I hope. We'll be as quiet as lambs."

"Coward," said one of Mr. Burke's companions as the earl walked back to join Harriet.

"Not I," said Mr. Burke. "There goes the best swordsman and shot in England."

That had the effect of reducing their subsequent conversation to a mumble.

"So," said the earl, "where are you bound?"

"To my sister, Mrs. Colville, who lives in Parton-in-the-Wold."

"An inclement time of the year to go traveling."

"My sister wishes me to bring out my niece at the Season. I have little wish to do so, and yet if I refuse, the whole family will descend on me. I thought it best to look the girl over first. She may be ugly."

He said with an edge of irritation in his voice,

"How like the cattle market you do sound! Look over the animal, if it is a handsome beast, it will do, if not, leave it."

"Ah, yes, I did sound like that," said Harriet in surprise. "But, you see, I do regard the Season as a sort of cattle market, and so I am apt to consider the pros and cons of bringing out a young miss by the rules of society. How dreadful to consider one of my sex in that light. I must think again. If the girl is plain, then she will be more in need of my services than if she commanded any sort of beauty at all. I am grateful to you."

She was quite plain herself, he thought. Her face was too thin and too clever-looking. But she had beautiful eyes and an exquisitely passionate mouth. She was not married. *Miss* Tremayne. Had anyone ever kissed that mouth?

"You must have bad memories of your own Season, Miss Tremayne, to be so harsh."

"I was fortunate enough not to have a Season."

Her clothes were plain but expensive. "And why was that?" he asked curiously.

"My parents died when I was on the verge of being brought out. Then a relative left me a substantial legacy, and so as I did not need to marry, I did not need to have a Season."

"Do you mean you would have married solely for money had you not received that legacy?"

"I would probably have been obliged to, my lord, for my father was a gambler and I would have been expected to repair the family fortunes. Mind you, I did not know my father had gambled most away until he died, but it was certainly being borne in on me before he did that only a gentleman with a

9

large fortune was going to be acceptable to him as a son-in-law."

"But once you had your independence," he said, pursuing the topic, "you could then pick and choose. Marry for love. Such a thing has been known."

Her green eyes sparkled with amusement. "You having married for love yourself, my lord?"

"Nearly. I was once engaged. She died."

"I am sorry."

"It was a long time ago, in my callow youth. Griselda was her name."

"As in the fairy tale?"

"Exactly." He leaned forward to embellish his tale further, wondering as he did so why he was going to such lengths to lie. "She had a sweet face and masses of golden hair and great blue eyes which looked at the world with a childlike wonder."

Harriet's empty soup plate had been taken away. She watched the earl as he drank his, at the firelight playing across the strong planes of his face. He did not look at all like the type of man to be so fascinated by a milk-and-water miss, which is what this Griselda sounded as if she had been. For the first time, Harriet was acutely aware of her spinster state, of the plainness of her clothes and face.

She waited until he had finished and said, "And so did you marry someone else?"

"No, Miss Tremayne. I found no other lady to match my Griselda."

Huffy was how Harriet was beginning to feel, but she put it down to a twinge of indigestion. The soup had been mulligatawny and highly spiced.

"But what of you, Miss Tremayne?" he asked, leaning back in his chair as his plate was removed.

10

"At your age, you must have come across some man who sparked your imagination."

How Harriet hated that remark "at your age." "I should estimate you are the same age as myself, my lord. But, no, it is not necessary to adore a man to be happy."

"So how do you pass your days?"

"I read and study a great deal and have female friends of like interests."

"Ah, bluestockings."

"That is how the sneer describes us, yes. I go to the opera and plays and concerts. I have a comfortable and happy life."

"Except when trapped in posting houses in snowstorms."

"Such a thing has not happened before. But it is hardly a desert island or even a blasted heath. It is a well-run posting house. Hardly an adventure."

The bloods at the other table had been drinking heavily. One of them suddenly vomited on the floor.

"This is enough," said the earl. "Miss Tremayne, we can *share* the private parlor, and to save your maidenly sensibilities, we will leave the door open. Come, I beg you. Things with that crowd will only get worse."

Harriet hesitated. Then she saw one rise and fetch a pot from the sideboard. If she stayed much longer, she might have to witness worse than vomiting.

"Thank you," she said, rising hurriedly.

"Go directly there, and I will instruct the landlord to bring our food upstairs."

Harriet fled.

She hesitated outside her maid's door—Lucy always had the luxury of her own bedchamber when

11

traveling with her mistress. She should ask the maid to chaperon her, but Lord Dangerfield would surely not allow a maid to sit at the table with them, and Lucy was probably asleep by now. She went on her way to the private parlor.

He joined her after a few moments. Now that she was alone with him in the little parlor, she was very conscious of his presence, of his masculinity. She reminded herself sternly that she was Miss Tremayne of independent means and not interested in gentlemen at all.

The waiters and the landlord entered, bearing dishes. "I took the liberty of ordering some wine for us," said the earl. "As I have taken your parlor away, I think it only fair that I should entertain you."

Harriet bowed her head. "You are most kind." She knew it would be churlish to protest. Even on stagecoach journeys, the male passengers paid for any female passengers' meals.

They ate in silence for a while, and then he said, "I wonder how long we will be trapped here?"

"Not long, I hope." Harriet stood up and went to the window, drew back the curtain, and peered out. "The snow is worse."

"Then it looks as if we are going to get to know each other very well." Harriet sat down again opposite him. The candle flames flickered and his eyes appeared to glitter. She felt uncomfortable and uneasy.

"Perhaps not, my lord. I am fortunate enough to have some books with me, so I shall spend the time in my room, reading."

"Without eating?"

"Of course not."

"Then we shall see each other at meals. Unless you plan to return to the dining room?"

Harriet repressed a shudder. "Not I. Can you imagine what it must be like to be married to one of those brutes?"

"Not being a female, that sad thought never crossed my mind. And you, being an independent bluestocking, need not concern yourself with such thoughts either ... unless, of course, you constantly look for things to justify your spinsterhood."

"That is cruel and untrue. I am happy and content with my life."

"With a mouth like that?"

"My speech offends you?"

"No, my sweeting. I merely remark that you have a passionate mouth."

"My lord, as we have been thrown into each other's company, may I beg you to refrain from making impolite personal comments."

"As you will. Some might regard it as a compliment."

"How far are you traveling, my lord?"

"To Oxford. I am to pay a visit to my old tutor."

"Did you attend the university, or is this gentleman a tutor of your youth who went with you on the Grand Tour?"

"I attended the university."

"And did you receive a degree?"

"Of course."

"Why of course?"

"I went out riding as usual with my tutor at the end of my stay. He asked me two easy questions to which I gave the correct answers and then he told me I had my degree."

"Is that customary?"

"My late father contributed funds to build a handsome library for the college. In such circumstances, yes, it is customary. Besides, the aristocracy cannot appear to fail."

"Women should be allowed to go to university."

"The next thing you will be saying is that they ought to have a vote."

"I do not see why not. We have minds, we have intelligence."

"That is not the general opinion."

"And what is the general opinion, as if I did not know?"

He smiled. "Women are the weaker sex, like children, put on this earth to please and support men and to bear them offspring."

"And that is what you believe? There are many such ladies who would agree with your description. Each Season abounds with debutantes who have been rigorously trained to think they are lesser creatures. So why haven't you married one?"

He gave her a limpid look. "You forget Griselda," he said sadly.

"Now, I do not believe that a man such as you has spent years pining away for a dead girl."

"You have a very unfeminine, ruthless streak, do you know that? Perhaps I should explain that once you have found true love, then nothing else will do."

"Perhaps you read too many romances, my lord."

"Not I. I am a gentleman of great sensibility."

"You are mocking me!"

"I am being truthful. Why will you not accept the truth of my statements? Is it because you do not want to?"

"My lord, if I did not want to believe your statements, it would be because I was romantically interested in you myself, which I most definitely am not."

Again he experienced that stab of pique that she could remain so indifferent to him.

"If you 'do' the Season with your young niece, then perhaps you yourself will find a mate."

Harriet laughed. "My lord, I will be seated with the other chaperones watching the success or otherwise of our protegées jealously. We will give tea parties and make calls to discuss which gentlemen are eligible, which are to be avoided. Will you be on such a list, or do you have a dreadful reputation that I should know about?"

"I have a dreadful reputation."

"And how can that be? Not with the ladies, surely?"

"Yes, with the ladies."

"You are not very faithful to Griselda's memory, then."

"I am. I am, I assure you. That is what makes me so fickle. No lady can match my Griselda."

"Life goes on," said Harriet sententiously. "You surely want heirs."

"My brother has four sons. There is no need for me to do my duty to secure the family line."

His eyes were mocking and she felt hot and uncomfortable. She was beginning to find his presence somewhat overwhelming. There was a silence as they both ate their food, and at the end of the meal, when the covers were removed, she rose to her feet with an air of relief. "I will leave you to your wine, my lord."

He walked with her to the door and then raised her hand to his lips and kissed it. Her hand trembled for a moment in his before she snatched it away. She dropped him a low curtsy.

"Until tomorrow, Miss Tremayne," he said softly.

Harriet walked to her room with a fast-beating heart. She went straight to the window and looked out. The snow had ceased to fall. She opened the window and leaned out. The air felt warmer and melting snow was already dripping from the eaves.

With any luck, she would be on her way tomorrow and would never have to meet the disturbing Lord Dangerfield again.

But the following day, although the snow was melting fast, the roads were considered too bad for traveling. Lord Dangerfield learned to his annoyance that Miss Tremayne was breakfasting in her room.

He walked around to the stables to talk to his coachman and groom and then returned to the still-silent inn. No one apart from the staff seemed to be awake.

He felt restless and bored, and then he remembered that Miss Tremayne had said she had brought books with her. Even some learned tome on the rights of women would do to alleviate the boredom of a snowbound inn, he thought, sending a waiter with a polite request that he might borrow a book.

The waiter returned with the first volume of Fanny Burney's *Evelina*. Surprised that the stern Miss Tremayne should read novels or even travel with them, he nonetheless settled down to read, expecting what he privately damned as the "usual female gothic rubbish." He was amused and de-

16

lighted, however, and by the afternoon sent the waiter back with a request for the second volume.

In between reading, he found he was looking forward to dinner immensely, rehearsing the things he would say to her to see if he could perhaps flirt with her a little and make her aware of him as a man.

But when he went to the private parlor, it was to find only one cover laid. "Where is Miss Tremayne?" he asked the landlord.

"We cleaned up another of the private parlors, the one that was to be painted, my lord, and took off the covers. Miss Tremayne and her maid are dining there."

He felt at first disappointed and then angry. Who was this Miss Tremayne to shun dining with an earl?

He ate his meal in gloomy silence, and then, returning to his room, collected the books and sent a waiter to her with them and a curt note of thanks.

His coachman waylaid him in the corridor to say that the roads were now clear enough for travel and with my lord's permission they would set off early in the morning.

He nodded, thinking that he would soon be shot of the place and with any luck he would never set eyes on that odd spinster again.

Chapter Two

HARRIET'S CARRIAGE JOLTED on its way. Watery winter sunlight gleamed in the puddles of melting snow in the surrounding fields. As she approached her sister's home, she searched in her bag for her steel mirror to make sure there were no smuts of dirt on her nose.

Her fingers encountered a stiff piece of paper. She drew it out. It was Lord Dangerfield's curt note thanking her for the loan of the books. She made to crumple it, planning to throw it away when she arrived, but instead, she put it back in her bag. It was a memento of a very odd meeting. She found herself reluctant to get rid of it.

Mary Colville lived in a rambling, low fourteenth-century house with many rooms, many stone floors, and not enough warmth. Harriet remembered it being cold even in midsummer and planned to stay only two nights. She wondered what illness Mary had found to "put on," for her sister dressed herself in various ailments with all the enthusiasm of a fashion-conscious dandy sporting a new waistcoat.

She was greeted by the butler and housekeeper and shown to her usual room. She was told that Mr. Colville had taken the younger children out skating but that madam was in the drawing room. Reflecting that only her absentminded brother-in-law would think of taking his children skating in the middle of a thaw, Harriet, with the help of her maid, changed out of her traveling clothes into a warm woolen gown and shawl and made her way to the drawing room on the ground floor, where thick carpets did little to stop the chill rising from the stone floor underneath. Harriet had suggested several times to Mr. Colville that he have the flags ripped out and replaced with wooden floors, but he would only smile vaguely and say, "Perhaps next year."

Mary Colville was lying on a daybed near the window. A table crowded with bottles of medicine was at her elbow.

"What is wrong, Mary?" asked Harriet.

"I fear I have a wasting illness," whispered Mary. "Come closer and let me look at you, Harriet. My sight fails me."

Remarkably sharp, beady eyes fastened on Harriet's face.

Knowing from long experience that it was useless to tell her sister she was actually as strong as an ox, Harriet drew a chair up to the daybed and sat down.

"I received your letter," said Harriet, "and am come to look at Susan, to get to know her. I have not seen her since she was a child. If I am to bring her out, then I must be sure that we will deal together tolerably well."

"You will have no trouble puffing her off," said Mary, forgetting to whisper. "She looks like an angel, has a fine dowry, and is all that is amiable."

"I am amazed, then, that you do not want to see her success yourself."

"Alas, I am not well enough. In fact, my dying wish is to see Susan settled."

"I do not think you are dying yet, Mary. When do I have the pleasure of meeting Susan?"

Mary fumbled with one thin white hand among the bottles on the table until she found a brass bell which she rang. When the butler answered, she asked him in a faint voice to fetch Miss Susan.

Harriet waited uneasily. There was a commotion outside. She went to the window and looked out. Mr. Colville was hurrying to the house, carrying one soaking-wet child, the rest trailing after him, their faces bright with excitement. She turned from the window.

"I think you will find that one of your children— Harry, I think—has fallen through the ice. Mr. Colville is carrying him into the house."

"Oh," said Mary.

"Do you wish me to go and see if he is well?"

"We have nurses and a governess," said Mary languidly. "That is what they are for."

The door opened and a vision walked in.

Dear heavens, thought Harriet. It's Griselda.

Susan Colville had a sweet, heart-shaped face and wide, innocent blue eyes. She had masses of fair curls, fine baby hair, and a perfectly shaped pink mouth. Her figure was dainty and her hands and feet small and delicately shaped. Despite the chill of the house, she was wearing a filmy white muslin gown.

"Welcome, Aunt Harriet," she said, dropping a curtsy.

"Come and kiss your mama," ordered Mary.

20

Susan tripped forward and dropped a butterfly kiss on Mary's face.

"Your aunt is to give you a Season," said Mary.

"I have not yet come to a decision." Harriet was alarmed and yet could not think why. Finding a husband for this dazzler would surely be the easiest thing in the world. She was beginning to find the "sickroom" oppressive. There was now an odd smell in it, as if of bad drains.

"Mama," said Susan. Her voice had a faint lisp. " 'Tis the Harveys' ball this night, and you said I might leave soon and stay with them."

"I had forgotten," said Mary. "How can your aunt see much of you if you are to go jauntering about?"

"But the Harveys' carriage is due to arrive for me any moment, and they will be mortally offended if I do not go. You did give your permission."

"Well, well. I suppose you must go."

"Thank you, Mama. I am in alt at meeting you, Aunt Harriet." Susan dropped a curtsy and left the room.

"Susan is uncommonly beautiful," said Harriet.

"And a beautiful nature." Mary appeared to rouse herself slightly. "You will bring her out, will you not, Harriet?"

Harriet hesitated. "I had planned to stay only a couple of days, Mary. But if Susan is to be absent, I cannot get to know her very well."

"There is nothing to know," said Mary. "She is as you saw her, sweet, charming, and beautiful. A very placid girl, too. Not one of your great hurly-burly creatures. 'Twould be best if you took her with you as soon as she returns from the Harveys, Harriet, for, as you can see, I am at death's door."

21

"In that case, perhaps Susan might do better to stay here and witness your last moments."

Mary threw her a haughty look. "You are hard and unfeeling as always, Harriet. It would comfort my last hours to know that my beautiful daughter was a success at the Season." She gave a little sigh and said in a more practical voice. "Susan doesn't really *notice* me, or indeed anyone else. I think she lives in another world."

Harriet felt trapped. The chill in the room was making her shiver. Two more days of this!

She excused herself and went in search of the butler and bribed him heavily to make sure a roaring fire was always burning in her bedchamber during her visit. Thank goodness for the books she had brought with her. She settled down to content herself with reading to pass the time.

By the time Susan returned, Harriet was more than ever eager to leave. Susan's little brothers and sisters were very noisy and spoiled and given to playing practical jokes. The night before, Harriet had had to rescue a bewildered hedgehog, fortunately still alive, from the bottom of her bed and carry it outside, where it could resume its hibernation.

In the flurry of packing and saying good-byes and arranging that Susan should take only the bare minimum of clothes, as she would need a much more fashionable wardrobe in London, she had little time for the girl herself.

It was only when they were in the carriage on the road home that she began to make an effort to get to know Susan.

"Are you looking forward to your Season?" she asked.

"Oh, yes," said Susan, giving her enchanting dimpled smile. "There will be lots to eat, will there not?"

"I keep a good table," replied Harriet.

"I mean at balls and parties. Lizzie Pomfret, one of my friends, told me they have all sorts of delicious ices and sugar plums."

"They do indeed. But ladies are expected to eat little, you know. Besides, you do not want to get fat and pimply."

"I never get fat or pimply," said Susan tranquilly.

"Would you like me to lend you something to read?"

"No, thank you. I never read."

"Why?"

"I cannot."

Harriet looked at those beautiful blue eyes.

"Do you need spectacles?"

"No, Aunt, my eyesight is very good."

"Then . . ."

"I never learned to read."

"*What?*"

"I said"—Susan stifled a yawn—"that I never learned to read. Such a bore."

"But you went to a seminary, surely?"

"Yes, of course. But the teachers did not pay me much heed. They liked to dress me up and display me on speech days and things like that."

"Can you write?"

Susan shook her head.

"But, my child, this is quite dreadful. You must begin your lessons immediately after we arrive.

23

How could your mother let such a state of affairs come about?"

"Well, you see, I am very beautiful, so I do not think it was considered necessary. Mama says that gentlemen do not like clever ladies."

"I do not think they like illiterate ones, either, Susan. You see, when you are married, you will be expected to be able to read your dressmaker's bills, at least. And have you thought what will happen when you lose your looks?"

"I will be married long before then and have lots and lots of doting children," said Susan placidly.

Harriet shook her head in bewilderment. "Did the other girls in that seminary leave without having learned anything?"

"Oh, I should not think so. They seemed awfully clever to me."

"I still cannot understand how you avoided learning anything."

She giggled. "I was so very ill, quite a lot. You cannot make an ill person learn. The teachers were very sympathetic."

"Surely they called a physician! And were you *pretending* to be ill?"

"Yes, it was all very simple. I went on just like Mama. Physicians *always* are happy to find something wrong with the rich."

"Do your parents know you cannot read or write?"

"I should not think so. They did not ask me."

Harriet felt quite low. The task of bringing Susan out, which had seemed so simple, was now beginning to look very difficult indeed. Then she wrinkled her nose and looked out the window to see if the carriage was passing any dung heap, but only wet fields stretched out in front of her view.

She looked at the soles of her shoes. "There is an awful smell," she said. "Lucy, Susan, look at your shoes."

But both ladies presented clean soles.

Then Harriet looked suspiciously at the glowing and beautiful Susan who was sitting so placidly beside her.

"Unfasten your cloak, Susan, and let me see your neck," she ordered.

Susan obediently unfastened the gold clasp that held her fur-lined cloak at the neck. "Take off your bonnet and tilt your head forward." Susan obediently did so. She had not yet begun to wear her hair up.

Harriet lifted the golden tresses. Susan's neck was gray and grimy. Her little ears were also dirty.

"When did you last have a bath, Susan?"

"I cannot remember. I wasn't really ill, you know, only pretending, so there was no need for baths," said Susan patiently, obviously believing like quite a large proportion of the population that bathing all over was only for the sick.

"But you must wash! You smell!"

"My clothes are laundered each week," said Susan, opening her eyes to their fullest, "and most people change their linen only every quarter day, or so I believe."

"Listen to me, miss, if you are to live with me, then you are going to have to be clean. Why is it your hair looks clean?"

"I brush it out regularly with Fuller's earth," said Susan proudly.

25

"That is not enough. Your hair must be washed in soap and water."

"But the dampness will affect my brain."

"It seems your brain has remained totally untouched. Soap and water, Susan, as soon as we break our journey."

Susan's surprise was almost comical. She said half to herself, "Mama did say you were a trifle eccentric, Aunt Harriet."

Harriet had chosen to stop at a different posting house on the return journey. She persuaded herself that the reason for this was that she was angry at the landlord for having failed to secure her that private parlor. But the real reason was buried away in the back of her brain. She simply would not admit that she was afraid of running into Lord Dangerfield again, when she was accompanied by a young lady who looked the very picture of the Griselda he had described.

So the carriage pulled in at the Bull, and Susan, to her bewilderment, found she was expected to take a bath and *wash all over* before sitting down to dinner.

A tin bath like a coffin was carried up to her bedchamber and filled with hot water. "Can you wash yourself?" asked Harriet.

"I think I can manage," said Susan completely without sarcasm.

"I will leave Lucy with you. She will dry you."

"The maid would see my naked body," said Susan in surprise. "I cannot be doing with that."

"Very well. But I expect you to be clean all over, and that includes your hair."

Susan washed herself, enjoying the novelty. She

26

also washed her hair thoroughly and dried it in front of the fire. Then she put on one of her filmy muslin gowns. Susan never felt the cold.

She brushed her curls, admiring the shine in the looking-glass and deciding that soap and water made a very effective cosmetic.

Satisfied with her appearance, she was just about to leave the room when she heard a commotion outside. She struggled with the catch of the casement window and leaned out. Four men were just arriving, their leader calling loudly to the ostlers to hold the horses' heads. They were all very fashionably dressed. Susan looked down at them curiously. Were these, then, London gentlemen? It was all very interesting.

And then one man saw the vision at the window and called to his friends. They all looked up at Susan, their mouths hanging open and dazed looks on their faces.

Susan thought they all looked very funny. She smiled and waved her hand and then closed the window and went along to the private parlor next door.

Harriet thought with a pang that Susan looked even more beautiful than before. "Aren't you cold?" she asked.

Susan shook her blond curls by way of reply and sat down at the table.

Dinner proved to be a fine spread. It consisted of fish in oyster sauce, boiled beef, roasted neck of pork with apple sauce, some hashed turkey, mutton steaks, salad, roasted wild duck, fried rabbits, a plum pudding, and tartlets.

But before they could begin this feast, the landlord entered with a waiter bearing a bottle of iced champagne. "What is this?" demanded Harriet. "I did not order champagne!"

"His lordship has sent it as a present."

"Which lord?" asked Harriet, her heart beating hard as she suddenly thought he must be referring to Lord Dangerfield.

"Lord Ampleforth, madam. He and his friends are desirous of presenting the champagne to the young lady."

Harriet's face hardened. "Take it away. We do not know Lord Ampleforth and do not wish presents."

When the landlord and the waiter had left, Harriet eyed Susan sharply. "Do *you* know this Lord Ampleforth?"

"Never heard of him." Susan eyed the food greedily. "This will all get cold, Aunt, if we do not begin."

"Begin by all means."

Susan fell to with a will, wielding her knife and fork like a trencherman.

"Do you always eat so much?" Harriet was just beginning, when she heard the sound of masculine voices raised in a love song coming from outside.

She went to the window and looked down. There were four young men there, one had a mandolin, and they were singing while staring up at the window.

She retreated hurriedly and sat down again.

Susan was now cramming food into her mouth with her fingers. "Don't do that," said Harriet sharply. "Susan, stop eating for just one moment and listen to me. There are four gentlemen below serenading, and I believe you must be the target, for it can hardly be me."

"No," said Susan with a giggle. "You are too old."

28

Oh, the heartlessness of youth, thought Harriet bleakly.

"They must have seen you, but how could they?" she asked.

"Four of them," said Susan, spearing a large piece of pork and cramming it into her mouth.

"Yes."

"Oh, 'em."

"I beg your pardon?"

Susan gulped down the pork and smiled sunnily at her aunt. "I heard people arriving before I came in to dinner, so I looked out the window and there were these four men all gaping up at me with such silly looks on their faces. I waved to them."

"You must never do that again," said Harriet, exasperated.

"It seemed only polite. I used to do that at the seminary. It was always so boring, don't you know, what with pretending to be ill and all, so sometimes I would wave out my window at people passing in the street and they were most kind and would send in poems and flowers and chocolates."

Harriet was horrified. "And did not the teachers stop these gifts from strangers?"

"Never saw them. I bribed the hall staff to smuggle them up to me. You see, it was the chocolates I liked. I wasn't allowed any of those in the seminary, and the staff would not go out and buy them for me for fear of being discovered. Shopkeepers are a gossipy lot."

"Susan, I am going to lecture you severely . . ."

Susan pointed her fork at her aunt. "If we are to deal together, you will find, Aunt Harriet, that I will listen to any stricture, but not when it comes between me and food."

"I will bide my time on this occasion," said Harriet.

But when pretty Susan appeared to have demolished everything in sight, burped, and wiped her mouth on the tablecloth, and Harriet proceeded to lecture her on maidenly behavior, Harriet had a shrewd idea that much as Susan liked to portray her teachers at the seminary as lax, she had heard all this before.

In the morning, when they set out, Lord Ampleforth and his friends were waiting in the courtyard. How they had managed to obtain bunches of hot-house flowers was a puzzle to Harriet. They pressed them on the delighted Susan, and Harriet could not bring herself to create a scene by making the girl refuse them.

"If only one of them had the wit to give me chocolates," mourned Susan as the carriage drove off.

"Oh, *Susan!*" exclaimed Harriet.

As soon as Susan was settled in London, Harriet decided to engage a tutor for her, feeling the girl might learn better from a stranger. To this end, she hired an elderly retired vicar to teach Susan to read and write, a music teacher to instruct her to play the pianoforte, a dancing master, and a seamstress to show her the fine art of sewing.

Having successfully managed to fill up the girl's days, she felt free to visit her friends. Her friends were also ladies of independent means. One of them, a Miss Barncastle, had prepared a lecture for them on the folly of fashion. As Harriet listened to Miss Barncastle pointing out the idiocies of the sisterhood having to paint themselves like savages and wear nigh indecent dresses and all to attract men, she glanced down at her own sober clothes and frowned.

She had not before been particularly conscious of her age and appearance. But having the ravishing Susan around had made her sharply aware of her declining years and dowdy clothes. She would need to order a new wardrobe for herself, she thought. She could not possibly take Susan to balls and parties in old-fashioned clothes. And perhaps she might indulge in one of the new fashionable crops. She caught a glimpse of her reflection in a looking-glass and scowled. She had hitherto chosen her bonnets to keep her head warm in winter and shade her from the sun in summer. The bonnet she was wearing was shaped like a coal scuttle and of dark felt. Susan had exclaimed, "What a quiz of a bonnet, Aunt Harriet! But then, I suppose when one is old, one does not need to bother about fashion." That had rankled.

But it *was* a quiz of a bonnet, thought Harriet, unaware that Miss Barncastle had come to the end of her lecture and all eyes were turned upon her, Harriet.

"Miss Tremayne," chided Miss Barncastle, "we are waiting to hear your views on the folly of fashion."

"I am not a good person to ask at the moment," said Harriet. "I have a young niece to bring out at the Season and that means I will need to help her choose gowns and all the frivolities. She is a good girl, but heedless and not interested in anything other than food. She would not understand my views."

34

Miss Barncastle raised her hands. "But you must teach her. How old is your niece?"

"Susan is nineteen."

"But it is your duty to school your niece, Miss Tremayne. We must save our sisters from becoming mindless chattels."

For the first time, Harriet felt like a stranger among them. She was worried about the responsibility of bringing out Susan and suddenly longed for the advice and help of someone in a similar situation. "Susan is quite happy to be a mindless chattel," she said. She raised a hand. "No, I do not wish to discuss the girl further. I must take my leave, ladies. I have much to do."

When she returned home to Berkeley Square, it was to find Susan sprawled out on the sofa with her gown hitched up and her face smeared with chocolate.

"Where is your dancing master?" demanded Harriet sharply.

"I'm learning," said Susan with an angelic smile.

"Learning what?"

"How to behave. I sent him away."

"Why?"

"He brought me these lovely chocolates, but then, when he was teaching me the waltz, he began to pant and his face turned red and he tried to kiss me."

Harriet sat down suddenly. Mr. Gerrard, the dancing master, had come with impeccable references.

Susan gave a yawn and then smiled. "Well, he *is* forty if he is a day, so I said he had to go away because I did not like being pawed by old men."

"And he went?"

"He burst into tears and ran away."

"I am sorry you have been subjected to such indignity. In the future when you have your dancing lessons, music lessons, or whatever, I will make sure one of my servants is always in the room. Perhaps you led him on, Susan. Your airs are a trifle too free and easy."

Susan swung her legs to the floor. "I thought it was only young men I had to be careful with."

"To put it as plainly and vulgarly as I can, you must be careful of anything in breeches from now on. Please go to your room and wash that chocolate off your face."

Susan tripped out. Harriet pulled the bell and told her butler to assemble all the servants. When they were all gathered, she told them that Miss Susan must never be left alone with any man, no matter what age, and she must never, ever be allowed to venture out on her own.

Then, having dismissed them, Harriet went to her desk and began to look through an old address book. Her face brightened as it fell on the name Bertha Tulloch. She had known Bertha when both were in their late teens. Bertha had been cheerful and worldly-wise even then. She had married before her first Season, a certain viscount, now, what was his name . . . ? Ah, Lord Dancer, that was it. She rang the bell and asked the butler to find out the direction of Lord Dancer and whether he was in town or not. After an hour, the butler returned with the intelligence that Lord Dancer resided in St. James's Square. Harriet ordered her carriage and went to change her gown, looking at the neat rows of unfashionable garments and suddenly wishing she had something more modish.

When she set out, she began to wish she had sent a footman around first with a note. Bertha might be much changed.

But Lady Dancer was at home and Harriet was ushered up to the drawing room. The pair surveyed each other in silence for a moment and then Bertha ran forward, holding out both hands. "Harriet, you have not changed a bit!"

"Nor you," said Harriet, "although you're vastly stylish."

"I am all the crack," said Bertha complacently.

She had changed, thought Harriet. She had grown slimmer, but her large eyes were as sparkling as ever and her brown hair under a lace cap just as thick and glossy.

"Tell me how you go on," urged Harriet. "Are you happy? Do you have children?"

"I have two boys, twins, both in the country with their tutor. And you? Are you still Miss Tremayne? I heard you had become a rich recluse."

"I lead a quiet life," said Harriet. "Or, rather, I *led* a quiet life. I should have called on you before and not waited until I needed your help."

"Tish! Of course I will help you."

"I have the onerous task of bringing out my niece, Susan Colville."

"And what is the problem? Little dowry? Face like a boot?"

"Large dowry and face like an angel. Men turn to jelly at the very sight of her."

"La! What is the problem?"

"Susan is lazy and does not like washing much. She is learning to read and write for the first time."

"You always did have frighteningly high standards, Harriet. Most of the cream of society are lazy and dirty and have minds totally untouched by learning."

"Come now, Bertha. The child must at least be fit to do household accounts."

"There, now. I can see you are worried."

"I am. The sad fact is that my friends are all equally spinsterish and bluestocking. I must enter the fashionable world. I need you to help me with clothes and jewels and frivolities."

Bertha clapped her hands. "We will have such fun, Harriet."

"You are so generous," said Harriet. "I confess the fair Susan has dampened my independent spirits. I am aware for the first time of being old."

"Fiddle! You are the same age as I. By the time I am finished with you, Harriet, you may be married yourself."

"Now, what gentleman in his right mind would want a woman like me? But there are all sorts of things I must do. Meet the hostesses, find out the eligibles."

"You will come with me on calls. But if this Susan is such a dazzler, we will not initially take her about with us. Many of the hostesses we will be meeting not only have eligible sons, but they have daughters to puff off and might not take kindly to the competition offered by a diamond of the first water like your Susan. As to eligibles . . ."

She crossed to a pretty little writing desk and took out a sheet of paper scrawled with spidery handwriting. "One of my friends who is bringing her daughter out this Season left this behind. I had been meaning to return it to her. It is a list of eligible men. Now, here is one, Charles Courtney. Quiet and stable and of good family, the Sussex

35

Courtneys. And there is Jeffrey Bland, a bit wild, but marriage would no doubt settle him. Of course, the most marriageable of all has decided to grace us this Season, but quite wicked, my dear, and perhaps too much of a man of the world for a little miss."

"And which gentleman might he be?" asked Harriet.

"Lord Dangerfield. The Earl of Dangerfield."

Chapter Three

HARRIET WENT SUDDENLY very still. Bertha rattled on. "Faith, he is a handsome creature."

"I . . . I met Lord Dangerfield."

"That must have been this age. He does not usually attend the Season."

"I met him when I journeyed to my sister's to collect Susan."

Bertha's eyes widened. "Tell me."

"There is nothing much to tell. I had booked a private parlor in a posting house to break my journey and, by some mistake, the same parlor had also been reserved for Lord Dangerfield. We ended up having dinner together."

"But this is wonderful! How romantic! How suitable for your Susan."

"He is a trifle old for Susan."

"Stuff. It never matters what age the gentleman is. A lady may be past any thought of marriage at his age. That is another matter."

There was a looking-glass behind Bertha. Harriet's reflection stared back at her, a dowdy, unmarriageable spinster. For one brief, mad moment when Bertha had exclaimed "How romantic," Harriet had thought that Bertha meant romantic for *her*, Harriet. But one look at her reflection showed her the folly of that thought. Not that she herself was in the remotest interested in such an uncomfortable man as Dangerfield. It was just that Bertha's dismissal of her as a marriageable prospect had made Harriet feel older than ever.

"I do not like the idea of Dangerfield for my Susan," she said firmly. "Apart from any considerations about age or experience, he is much too intelligent for my dim-witted Susan."

"I think it is you who are sadly lacking in worldly wisdom, Harriet. When did any gentleman, no matter what his intelligence, fail to be seduced by the sight of a pretty girl?"

"Perhaps you have the right of it," said Harriet, "but I shall do everything in my power to find Susan a suitable gentleman, and I do not consider Lord Dangerfield at all suitable."

"He has the reputation of being a heartbreaker, but all gentlemen settle down sooner or later."

"I would rather not discuss him."

Bertha looked at her curiously, but then she said, "Perhaps the best thing I can do for you is to get my bonnet and go with you to see Susan."

"How good you are. And clothes! How much I need your advice on clothes."

"And you will have it. *En avant!*"

The following weeks passed in a flurry of shopping and being fitted and pinned. Harriet had never bothered to buy any jewelry before, but she purchased a diamond tiara and necklace for herself. There was no need to buy expensive jewels for Susan. Debutantes were expected to sport only a simple coral necklace or string of pearls. In all the fuss, she did not have time to call on her bluestock-

38

ing friends and occasionally felt guilty about neglecting them. But somehow, once Harriet had the bit between her teeth, she could not stop. As her own new wardrobe arrived, she threw away all her old clothes, or, rather, she gave everything she had to Lucy so that the maid could take what she wanted and give the rest to the other servants to wear or sell. The next great expense was a smart phaeton so that when the weather turned fine, Harriet could take Susan to the park. Harriet was an excellent whip and could drive herself.

She went with Bertha to visit various ladies of the ton now dressed fashionably and with her dark hair in one of the new crops. Harriet did not know quite how much her new hairstyle had altered her appearance, making her look younger and her fine eyes bigger. Perhaps she might have begun to feel at least comfortable with her changed appearance had not her friends, headed by Miss Barncastle, decided to pay her an impromptu visit. They were waiting for her one day when she returned after a successful visit to the Marchioness of Trowbridge, having secured invitations for herself and Susan to that lady's pre-Season ball.

As Harriet entered her drawing room, where they were all seated, the ladies looked in amazement at the fashion plate that Harriet had become.

Miss Barncastle was the first to speak. She looked sternly at Harriet. "You have joined *them*," she said accusingly.

Harriet stripped off her gloves and said impatiently, "Would you have me try to sponsor a young female into the fashionable world while looking like a dowd?"

"You should have stuck to your principles," said another, a Miss Teale.

Harriet looked at them uneasily. They had all prided themselves on being such intellectuals, and the fact that any man might view them as just a lot of embittered spinsters added to their determination to keep to their views, to stick together. Women such as themselves spurned the fripperies of fashion.

She said mildly, "I hardly think it fair to inflict my views on a young lady who only looks forward to balls and parties and beaux." Harriet reflected that Susan probably looked forward only to the delicacies she could manage to cram into her beautiful mouth at such functions.

She also reflected for the first time that some of the most famous of the bluestockings, ladies she had never met, were happily married. But she felt a traitor and wished they would all go away.

The conversation was stilted. Miss Barncastle had submitted an article to the *Ladies Magazine* and it had been rejected, which all went to show that it was probably run by men.

"But we have all admired the articles in the *Ladies Magazine* and had often read them aloud," protested Harriet.

Miss Barncastle bridled. "Are you saying my work was probably not good enough?"

"No, no, not at all," said Harriet miserably. The visit became worse when Miss Teale said they would all be happy when the Season was over and they got their "dear Harriet" back, "for you look not at all like yourself with that odd haircut."

Susan had entered the room during the last of the conversation. She was carrying a box of chocolates. She was introduced all around. She smiled at everyone vaguely and then went and curled up on the window seat while Harriet sweated her way through pleasantries until it was time for the ladies to take their leave.

Harriet returned to the drawing room after saying good-bye to the guests and sat down with a little sigh. She had forgotten all about Susan until a voice from the window seat remarked, "What a jealous lot of frumps."

"Susan! I had forgotten you were there. Do not be rude about my friends."

"No friends of yours. You may think me stupid and ill educated, Aunt, but with my looks there is one thing I have come to recognize and that is jealousy."

"Why on earth would they be jealous of me?"

"Oh, take a look at yourself. You are not pretty or beautiful, but I would say you are now a vastly modish and attractive-looking lady."

"Why, thank you, Susan." Harriet studied herself cautiously in the glass. "Do you really think so?"

"Yes, you know I never say what I do not think."

For the first time, Harriet felt a warm glow of pure affection for her niece.

Lord Dangerfield returned to London to find piles of invitation cards waiting for him. The fact that he was to attend the Season had obviously got about. He flipped through them, wondering in a way why he was bothering, why he had suddenly decided to find a wife. He debated whether to call on his mistress or go to his club. His mistress was a widow, Mrs. Verity Palfrey, of good ton and loose morals. His arrangement with her had lasted for two years.

He decided to go to his club.

The first person he saw in the coffee room was Viscount Ampleforth, who was looking with loathing at a glass of seltzer.

"Bad head?" asked the earl sympathetically.

"The worst." Ampleforth looked up at him with bloodshot eyes. "Love and liquor don't mix."

The earl sat down and stretched out his long legs. "What is this, Ampleforth? Do you need the advice of an older man?"

"Not in this case," said Lord Ampleforth gloomily. He took a sip of seltzer and shuddered. "I ain't talking about wenching, I'm talking about love, pure love, all that stuff the poets maunder on about."

"Dear me, and who is this paragon of virtue who has stolen your heart?"

"Miss Susan Colville."

"Never heard of her."

"She is new to town. But I met her last January at a posting house. She is a divine angel but guarded by a frump of a dragon called Miss Harriet Tremayne."

"Miss Tremayne is known to me, Ampleforth, and you will speak of her with respect in the future, or I shall have to call you out."

"Forgive me. I caught only a glimpse of the drag—of Miss Tremayne when she and the divinity were leaving in the morning. The light was bad. Forgive me. But this is splendid! If you are acquainted with Miss Tremayne, perhaps you can get me an introduction."

"I know Miss Tremayne only slightly and do not know where she resides."

"In Berkeley Square, about five doors along from Gunter's. One of her servants told my man that Miss Tremayne has bought a new phaeton and is to take Miss Colville out this very afternoon driving in the park. Perhaps we could go together and you could introduce me there."

"Sorry, Ampleforth, I have other things to do."

"You might help out a despairing fellow!"

"You will see plenty of your charmer at the Season."

"I won't get near her," said Lord Ampleforth gloomily.

The earl spent some hours talking to friends, having a boxing session at Gentleman Jackson's Saloon in Bond Street, and choosing material for a waistcoat. It was only when he noticed the time on a church clock and registered that the fashionable hour for driving in Hyde Park—five o'clock—was not far off that he was suddenly overcome with curiosity to see the formidable Miss Tremayne again.

He went home quickly and ordered his carriage to be brought around from the mews and set off in the direction of the park.

At first Harriet was enjoying the pleasure of tooling her smart new phaeton too much to realize what a sensation Susan, in blue muslin and chip straw hat embellished with flowers, was causing. But once she turned smartly in at the gates of the park she became aware of the commotion Susan's appearance was creating. Gentlemen were standing up precariously in their carriages to get a better look. Susan recognized Lord Ampleforth and smiled radiantly and he clutched his heart. His horse backed suddenly and he fell back in his carriage with his feet in the air. Harriet assumed Su-

43

san had remembered Lord Ampleforth from the inn courtyard, but Susan, sitting by the window when Harriet was out on calls, had seen him walking past almost every day.

Harriet felt a lot of her anxieties easing. Susan would surely be engaged to be married almost as soon as the Season started, and then she could return to her old ways. Yet, she was enjoying her new clothes and her busy social life, but the last visit from her friends was a sour memory. Could it be that she, the intelligent and independent Miss Tremayne, had been deluding herself? She had an uneasy feeling that the *real* bluestockings might find them all rather pathetic. But all this did was to give her a stab of disloyalty. She had spent many happy hours with Miss Barncastle and the rest.

And then she saw a gentleman driving toward her and promptly forgot about anyone and everything else. It was Lord Dangerfield. He slowed his team to a halt, and Harriet reined in her horse so that both carriages were alongside each other. He raised his hat. "Miss Tremayne, I hardly recognized you," he said.

"Am I so much changed?"

"Very much for the better."

He looked at Susan and gave a slow smile. "Will you not introduce me to Griselda?"

Harriet's heart plunged sickeningly. "My niece, Miss Susan Colville, Susan, Lord Dangerfield."

Susan flashed that brilliant smile of hers.

"London has seen nothing like you, Miss Colville," said the earl. "You are already breaking hearts right, left, and center."

"So it would appear," said Susan with her faint lisp. "Do you think I will be all the rage?"

"Undoubtedly."

"Then, that is good. For my aunt will get me off her hands very soon and she can be comfortable again. Aunt Harriet is not of a frivolous nature."

His eyes sparkled with laughter. "Is Miss Tremayne *very* strict?"

"Oh, no. But Aunt Harriet has had a most fatiguing time what with having to teach me to read and write and choose clothes for me and go on calls and all that sort of thing."

"You could not read and write before your aunt took you in hand?"

Susan gave a gurgle of laughter. "No, is it not shocking?"

"So now that you are literate and modishly gowned, all you have to do is look forward to all the balls and parties."

"I suppose so. We are to go to the Marchioness of Trowbridge's ball. Does she keep a good table?"

"Very good, Miss Colville."

"Susan," muttered Harriet warningly, but Susan appeared not to hear.

"I mean, does she have good confectionery?"

"Gunter's will probably be doing the catering, and there will be ices and all sorts of delights."

"Then I shall look forward to it. And you must dance with Aunt Harriet, my lord, for she has such a pretty ball gown and will look much too dashing to be confined to the rows of dowagers and chaperones. Besides, you and Aunt are of an age, I should think."

"It will be my pleasure," said the earl, ignoring the fulminating looks Harriet was casting on her niece. "I shall call on you, Miss Tremayne."

He touched his hat and drove on.

45

"Susan!" said Harriet furiously. "Never again so-
licit any gentleman to give me a dance, and never,
ever comment on his age."

Susan sighed. "Such a lot to learn," she said.
"Had we not better move on? Have you noticed how
everyone stares? Most rude."

But another carriage had stopped beside them.
Harriet recognized Mrs. Courtney, one of the hostesses Bertha had encouraged her to cultivate. A
pleasant-looking young man was with her. Mrs.
Courtney introduced him as her son, Charles.

After some bland exchanges of conversation, during which Susan remained mercifully silent,
Harriet finished by saying she would be delighted
if Mr. Courtney and his mother would call on her.
She then drove Susan briskly once around the Ring
and thankfully made her way home, wondering
why her mouth was dry and why her heart was
beating so hard. Stage nerves, she told herself severely. After the marchioness's ball, Susan would
be firmly on her way to marriage and all she,
Harriet, had to do was to choose a suitable husband for the girl. Young Courtney would be ideal.
He was only a couple of years older than Susan and
he appeared good-natured and amiable.

But worries about Susan surfaced again. For as
soon as they returned home, Susan tossed her bonnet into a corner, dropped her pelisse on the drawing room floor, stretched her length on the sofa,
and fell fast asleep. Harriet gave a click of annoyance. Certainly she had planned no evening engagement. The Trowbridge ball was to be Susan's
first evening debut in society. But she had pianoforte scales to practice and more reading and writing to do. Susan's ability to fall fast asleep at any

46

given moment of the day bewildered the energetic Harriet.

Then there was the problem of Lord Dangerfield. Certainly he had not seemed struck all of a heap by Susan's beauty. But he had said he would call, and Susan appeared to amuse and delight him. Bertha had told Harriet that Lord Dangerfield had a mistress, quite as if that were an everyday sort of thing. In her brain Harriet knew it was; in her heart she felt it diminished him.

Ladies of the ton had two main functions in life. One was to produce an heir and spares and the other, having raised the children to marriageable age, was to find husbands for the girls and brides for the sons. The master of the house stepped in to discuss marriage settlements. Girls had to be guided away from adventurers and sons from ladies who lacked suitable dowries. The Regency was an age of hard gambling, and therefore it was more important than ever to keep the family finances afloat by marrying well.

So it quickly went around that not only was Susan Colville surpassingly beautiful but possessed of a handsome dowry. Had she had little money, then her fair looks would have been branded as blowsy and unfashionable. But the men saw her as a goddess and the matchmaking mamas viewed her as a sweet, amiable girl who could be easily molded to the family's ways.

So when Charles Courtney called the following afternoon, he was accompanied by his mother, his father being submerged in an armchair at his club with a bottle of burgundy.

Harriet sent the servants to fetch Susan and

looked up in dismay when her butler returned to say that Miss Susan could not be found.

Then Lord Dangerfield arrived to find Harriet flustered and upset. She sharply told the butler to go and look for Susan again and search the house from attic to cellar. But again he returned and said there was no sign of her.

Mrs. Courtney and Charles took their leave. Lord Dangerfield looked at Harriet with some amusement. "Do not force yourself to make polite conversation with me, Miss Tremayne. You are obviously worried to death about your niece. Ask the servants if any of them saw her recently and where."

Harriet rang the bell and questioned the butler. He withdrew and returned a few minutes later with a shamefaced footman who said that Susan had given him money to go out and buy chocolates for her. He had delivered the chocolates to her room.

When the servants had gone, Harriet said in a voice sharp with exasperation, "I told her that she must give up eating sweetmeats. She will destroy her complexion and her teeth."

"In that case," said Lord Dangerfield, "she probably found a hiding place where she could eat the chocolates without you coming down on her like the wrath of God. Come. Take me to her room. I do not share your worry and so can probably guess where she is. I feel she is hiding in the house, but it is clear to me that you are panicking and cannot think clearly because you fear she is wandering the streets of London."

Harriet hesitated. "Come along," he urged. "You must look on me as a friend of the family. After all, we have shared dinner and books."

She led him up to Susan's bedchamber. He stood in the doorway and looked around. There was a canopied bed, a toilet table, two easy chairs, a large wardrobe, and an even larger press.

As they stood together, looking around, a faint sound came from the press.

"Ah-ha!" He went and opened the door. Curled up on a shelf, her face smeared with chocolate, her thumb in her mouth, and fast asleep, lay Susan.

Harriet's first feeling was of mild pleasure that this beauty should display herself to such disadvantage. She then told herself sternly that this was not because the girl had been discovered by Lord Dangerfield in such a state, but simply pleasure at finding her safe and well.

"Susan!" she said sharply. "Come out of there immediately."

Susan slowly opened her beautiful eyes and blinked at Harriet and the earl. She unstoppered her mouth and grinned. "Now I am in the suds," she remarked. She slid down from the shelf, and as she did so, her dress rode up, revealing a splendid pair of legs encased in silk stockings and embellished with pink frilly garters.

"Wash your face, miss," said Harriet, "and present yourself in the drawing room. Mrs. Courtney has already called with Charles. It's too bad of you, Susan. You must stop eating so many sweetmeats. You will ruin your complexion and your teeth."

Susan yawned and stretched. "I never get pimples," she said. "And my teeth are very strong. Yes, yes, Aunt, do take your beau away and I will join you as soon as I can."

Harriet's face flamed with angry color. "Lord Dangerfield is *not* my beau, Susan. What am I to do with you? Make yourself presentable as soon as possible. Come, Lord Dangerfield."

When she and the earl were seated in the drawing room, Harriet said awkwardly, "I must apologize for my niece, my lord. As you can see, I have much work still to do."

He laughed. "And I thought *you* were the Original. I never thought to see you behave like the veriest model of society matrons." And Harriet felt staid and old and dowdy. She made rather stilted conversation, wondering why he did not take his leave. Calls were supposed to last only ten or fifteen minutes, and the time was stretching on to a full half hour. She made rather forced conversation about who was who at the Season and saying that Lady Dancer had been a great help in introducing her to the right hostesses.

"My lord," she said at last. "I am afraid you must excuse me. I do not know what can have happened to Susan."

"May I make a guess? Asleep again?"

"Surely not! I am sure she is making an elaborate toilet in your honor."

"Nicely said, Miss Tremayne. But I wager you that she is asleep."

"She cannot be!"

"You will find I have the right of it. What will we wager? I know, if I am right, then you will save the supper dance for me at the Trowbridge ball. And if I am wrong . . . ?"

"Well, well, I must think of something."

"Jewels? A fan?"

"No, I have enough of those. I know, you must give me your advice."

"On what?"

"On a suitable partner for Susan. I have been out of the world for so long. My friend, Bertha, Lady Dancer, is very shrewd, but perhaps you would be able to spot someone unsuitable better than she. There are gentlemen of good fortune who might be cruel, or drunkards, or gamblers. Gentlemen appear to be on their best behavior when they are courting. But a man would know what they are really like."

"Done! So let us go and see which of us is right."

They went back up to Susan's bedchamber. Harriet scratched at the door and then quietly opened it. Susan lay sprawled like a rag doll facedown on the bed and fast asleep again.

"The supper dance is mine, I think," said the earl.

"What on earth am I to do with her?" wailed Harriet.

"Make sure she stays awake in the ballroom," he said, "and let her beauty do the rest." His harsh face softened as he looked at the sleeping Susan. "She is quite the most beautiful girl I have ever seen."

"I think young Charles Courtney might be highly suitable," said Harriet.

His eyes glinted down at her. "Perhaps an older man might be what she needs."

Harriet led the way out of the bedroom. "I do not think so," she said over her shoulder, trying to keep her voice light. He followed her to the drawing room and she wondered just how long he meant to stay. She found him disturbing and unsettling and had a sudden sharp longing for the quiet, placid days of her old life.

"Come for a drive with me, Miss Tremayne," he said suddenly.

"Now?" She glanced at the clock. "It is not yet the fashionable hour."

"We do not need to be fashionable. See, the sun is shining and it is quite warm."

"But, Susan . . ."

"Miss Colville will no doubt sleep happily until our return. Besides, how can I present myself as a correct suitor if I do not gain your approval?"

She looked at him, startled. She wanted to cry out that never would she let such an experienced man of the world marry Susan. But Bertha and everyone else would think her quite mad to turn down anyone so eligible.

And yet she found herself accepting his invitation. She murmured that she would change into her carriage dress.

The earl nodded by way of reply and settled down to wait. The drawing room was restful, he thought. The long windows were open and a faint breeze stirred the lace curtains and sent them billowing out over the polished floor. There was a jar of potpourri on a side table giving out a pleasant scent, an apple-wood fire burned on the hearth, the clock ticked, and he had a feeling of being at home. He reflected that he had done nothing at all to the town house, or the country mansion, for that matter, leaving the pictures and furniture of his ancestors in place. His eyes roamed around the room again. There was a bowl of flowers, prettily arranged, and a piece of sewing lying on top of the work basket, books and magazines on a console table. A place to come home to. He was overcome by a temptation to flirt with the severe Miss Tremayne. He wondered idly what it would be like to kiss that passionate mouth and see those magnificent eyes of hers cloud with desire.

Harriet returned very quickly—he had expected her to take at least an hour, but she had been gone only fifteen minutes. She was wearing a carriage gown of gold velvet and a smart gold velvet hat, very small, tilted on one side of her head. Her hair, he noticed, was thick and curly and glossy.

"Where are we going?" asked Harriet when she was seated beside him in his carriage. He stretched his long, booted legs against the spatterboard and turned and smiled down at her. "Oh, just about. Here and there."

He set the horses in motion. They drove smartly out of Berkeley Square. Harriet felt a sudden surge of exhilaration. As he made his way through the press of traffic in Piccadilly and then slowed as he found his way blocked by a government sledge surrounded by soldiers taking the national lottery to the Bank of England, he said, "Who are those ladies glaring at you? Do you know them, or have complete strangers suddenly taken you in dislike?"

He pointed with his whip.

Miss Barncastle and another member of the sisterhood, Miss Carrington, were standing at the edge of the pavement, glaring at Harriet.

She waved and smiled. They gave little half waves back, but looked at her with condemnation in their eyes.

"So you do know them," commented the earl.

"Yes, they are dear friends of mine."

"Indeed! And do all your dear friends look at you as if you had just risen from hell and smelled of brimstone?"

53

Harriet gave a reluctant laugh. "I fear they find me much changed."

"In what way?"

"They fear I am become sadly frivolous."

"I cannot think of anyone less frivolous, Miss Tremayne. Who exactly were those ladies?"

"A Miss Barncastle and a Miss Carrington. Before the advent of Susan, I would visit with them and similar ... similar ..."

"Spinsters?"

"Yes, but we would discuss books and articles and the rights of women."

"But they must realize that such intellectual visits are put aside when one has a young female to launch upon the Season."

"I think it is my changed appearance that offends them. They fear I am become sadly fashionable."

"Ah, they are jealous."

"But why? They are all independently wealthy. They can all afford the best of clothes and jewels."

"They cannot buy your appearance, Miss Tremayne, or your grace of figure, your fine eyes, or your mouth."

"You put me to the blush," said Harriet severely. She tried to tell herself that such compliments were all part of social intercourse and never to be taken seriously, but she felt a warm glow start somewhere inside her. London seemed like a magic city. Sunshine gilded the roofs and buildings. The striped blinds over the windows of the houses fluttered in the wind.

"Where are we going?" she asked.

"There is a tea garden in Chelsea by the river. Have you been there?"

"No, I hardly ever venture as far as Chelsea."

"Your friends would approve." His eyes mocked her. "No one frivolous or fashionable goes there, but the setting is pretty and it is not often that one gets a day as fine or as warm at this time of the year."

The garden was as pretty as he had described it, with tables set out on the grass under the trees and with a fine view of the river.

"So what will you do, Miss Tremayne, when Miss Colville is safely off your hands? Is she an orphan?"

"No, you have forgotten. When you met me I was on my way to my sister's to collect Susan."

"And why cannot the fond mama bring her out?"

"My sister does not enjoy the best of health and I gather the Season can be very fatiguing."

"So what will you do when it ends?"

"Return gratefully to my quiet life."

"And your grim friends?"

"They are not grim!"

"True friends support one in all that one does, Miss Tremayne. In my humble opinion, had they been true friends, then they would have been helping you in your quest for a suitable husband for Miss Colville, not standing in Piccadilly, glaring at you."

"You do not understand!"

"No, and I hope I never do. I know Lady Dancer. You mentioned her as being a friend of yours. Now, she appears all that is amiable."

"Yes, she is very kind and has given up a great deal of her time to help me."

"Perhaps you will make new friends. Have you considered that you yourself might marry?"

"I think we have discussed me enough. What

about you, my lord? Are you really interested in marrying Susan?"

He looked at her in surprise. "Did I say so?"

"Oh, yes, that is the reason for this drive. You wish to ingratiate yourself with me so that your suit will be welcome."

For a brief moment his eyes flashed with anger and she looked back at him, puzzled. Then his face cleared and he laughed. "I have never yet met a woman with less vanity than you, Miss Tremayne. Now, I, I have my modicum of vanity. When I was a boy, I used to pray that I would wake up one morning with hair as black as your own. Red hair is so unfashionable."

Harriet looked at his dark red hair. "Yet you wear it unpowdered."

"Ah, you see, I am hoping someone will love me truly despite my red hair." He smiled into her large green eyes. "Do you think, Miss Tremayne, that a lady could love me for myself alone?"

"Many ladies would find it easy to love you, my lord."

"Why? Pray tell me."

"Your title and your fortune."

"A sore wound, Miss Tremayne. You are supposed to say because of my striking looks."

She gave a little sigh. "It is a wicked and mercenary world we live in. Despite her beauty, little Susan would be hard put to find suitors if she lacked a dowry."

"She is so very beautiful, I think someone would want to marry her even if she had no fortune at all."

"If they can find her awake enough to propose."

"It would be a simple matter. A box of the very

best chocolates and little Miss Susan would fall into anybody's arms."

"Oh, dear. Perhaps you can tell me which gentlemen are to be at the Season that she should be protected against . . . apart from you yourself."

"Now, why should Miss Colville be protected from me?"

"She is very young and . . . and . . . pure and you keep a mistress."

His face darkened. "The day becomes chilly," he said. "Shall we go?"

Harriet bit her lip, wondering what had possessed her to make such a disgraceful remark. If Susan were to be kept from all the men in London who kept mistresses or visited whores, then she would have very few to choose from.

They drove in silence to Hyde Park toll, where they joined a queue of carriages. A smart little curricle lined with quilted white silk drew alongside. It was driven by a buxom brunette with dark, liquid eyes. She was dressed in the first stare of fashion.

"Dangerfield," she called. "Where have you been? I have not seen you this age."

He bowed and said, "I will call on you presently," and then the carriages moved on.

"You did not introduce me," said Harriet in a small voice.

"Naturally not," he remarked in an icy voice.

Harriet felt very low. She was sure the stylish lady was the earl's mistress.

Harriet found Bertha waiting for her in the drawing room. "What is this, you sly puss?" cried

Bertha. "I have just heard from London's greatest gossip that you were seen this day being driven by Dangerfield and that he seemed very happy in your company."

Sighing, and untying the strings of her bonnet, Harriet said wearily, "Lord Dangerfield is cultivating my company with a view to courting Susan."

"Oh, tish and fiddlesticks. He would have been so suitable for you. Is it not lowering when a man like Dangerfield waits this age to get married and then falls for some milk-and-water miss?"

"Well, as you first pointed out to me, men of Dangerfield's age are marriageable, women of my age are not."

"But you are so changed, so modish! Oh, it is all too bad."

"Does . . . does Dangerfield have a mistress? Did you not say so? When we were making that call on the Marchioness of Trowbridge, I believe she said something to that effect."

"He has a liaison with Mrs. Verity Palfrey. Do you know her?"

Harriet looked startled. "Why should I know such a creature?"

"She is very good ton. In fact, she was considered highly respectable at one time. Palfrey was considerably older than she. Very rich. He died of an apoplexy. Up till then, she had seemed such a quiet creature, but then she began to appear everywhere in rather shocking gowns—damped muslin, my dear—Roman sandals, and toenails stained with cochineal. Do you know Sir Thomas Jeynes?"

"No."

"She had a passionate affair with him, and then

58

two years ago she switched to Dangerfield. You *have* been out of the world for too long. 'Twas a monstrous scandal. Jeynes challenged Dangerfield to a duel, pistols in Hyde Park at dawn. Dangerfield is a first-class shot and merely winged him in the arm. The seconds said he could easily have killed him."

"Oh," said Harriet in a little voice. She could never in her wildest fantasies imagine two men fighting over *her*.

"So how goes the fair Susan?"

"As usual. Which means I am increasingly worried about her. Young Courtney came to call with his mother, eminently suitable, and she was nowhere to be found. Then Dangerfield called and wagered me he could find her. Can you believe this, Bertha? Susan was fast asleep on a shelf of the press in her room with her thumb in her mouth. She had been eating chocolates again."

Bertha looked shrewdly at Harriet. "And what was the wager?"

"That I would save the supper dance for him at the Trowbridge ball."

"And then he took you driving for all the world to see! Hardly the behavior of a man who is enamored of your niece."

"He *told* me," said Harriet, "that he wanted to get into my good books with a view to courting Susan."

"And that's *exactly* what he said?"

"I cannot remember the exact words, but that is the sum and substance of them."

"And what do you feel about Dangerfield for your niece, now that you know him better?"

"I do not think him at all suitable."

Bertha looked down and played with the sticks of her fan. "Now, why did I think you would say that?"

Chapter Four

HARRIET WAITED UNEASILY in the drawing room for Susan to make an appearance. They were about to set off for the Trowbridge ball. Harriet was wearing a dark green silk gown of a modish cut. She felt uneasily that the neckline was a trifle too low, but the dressmaker had said it was the latest fashion. On her head was the new diamond tiara and she had a fine diamond necklace about her neck. Her gloves were of lighter green kid, as were her little dancing slippers. She had fretted over the great question of whether to paint or not to paint. How many times had she and her friends jeered at society women who smeared their faces like savages. But the realization that her cheeks were a trifle pale had made her apply a little rouge, although with a guilty feeling that she was betraying some important cause. She worried, too, that she had wasted too much time, effort, and money on bedecking herself. All eyes would be on Susan and she would have to content herself with sitting with the other chaperones and mothers against the wall. But Lord Dangerfield had said he would take her up for the supper dance.

When Susan walked into the room followed by Harriet's lady's maid, Harriet thought that once the gentlemen in the room saw Susan, her own existence would be forgotten.

Susan was wearing a thin white muslin gown with little puffed sleeves, a low neckline, and flounces of muslin that frothed around her ankles like white foam. A coronet of silver roses ornamented her hair, and she wore a white overdress of silver-spangled gauze. Her only ornament was a thin string of seed pearls about her neck. Her wide blue eyes shone and her complexion, despite a constant diet of sweetmeats, was flawless.

Mr. Charles Courtney was to escort them, and when he entered the room shortly after Susan and Harriet saw the way he gazed adoringly at the girl, she felt a surge of triumph. With any luck, young Courtney would propose quite soon, and then all her worries would be over.

So this, then, thought Harriet, would be her own first London ball. For the very first time she felt a little nagging pang that she was so old. Her very fear of marriage had made her miss a lot of fun, she thought wistfully.

But what was the alternative? The chattel of some man and years and years of childbearing.

As she walked up the red Turkey carpeted stairs to the ballroom at the Marchioness of Trowbridge's Grosvenor Square home, Harriet glanced at Susan beside her and felt a rush of sheer pride. The girl was exquisite.

There were many in the crowded ballroom who had heard of Susan but not yet seen her. Everyone simply stared, quite openly, many fumbling for their quizzing glasses to get a better look.

Charles Courtney led Susan into the first dance and Harriet found a seat behind some potted palms. Through the leaves she could catch glimpses of Susan and yet be partially screened and not feel obliged to make conversation. She was very surprised to find a young captain, therefore, bowing before her and asking her to dance. Feeling slightly startled, she accepted and joined a set for the quadrille just as the dance started. Harriet had been taught by an excellent dancing master but at first was frightened she might have forgotten the steps. However, she performed very well and found she was enjoying herself. The captain, when they were promenading after the dance, introduced himself as Captain Preston and, to Harriet's surprise, escorted her back to her chair and went to fetch her a glass of lemonade. He had returned with it and one for himself and was drawing forward a chair to sit down next to Harriet, when Lord Dangerfield walked into the ballroom.

His eyes rested curiously on Harriet and her young gallant, and then he was lost to her view.

"You are the aunt of Miss Colville, London's latest beauty, are you not?" asked the captain.

"Yes," said Harriet with a sympathetic smile. She felt perfectly sure this captain was cultivating her company with a view to getting to know Susan. "I am very proud of her. She looks very well."

Captain Preston's eyes rested on Harriet's face. "Such dazzlers make me feel uncomfortable. I would rather sit here with you and drink a toast to your beautiful emerald eyes."

"Sir, you flatter me."

"I tell only the truth. But I am not going to enjoy your company for very much longer. Here comes Lord Moulton."

To Harriet's increasing bewilderment, she was

led off to dance the waltz by Lord Moulton, who she judged to be also much younger than herself. He was a tall, gangly young man, quite shy, who blushed furiously when he put his hand at her waist, and so Harriet, who had never danced the waltz with anyone but her dancing master, felt suddenly happy and confident. She could not believe she was actually dancing and having fun. She wondered who Susan's current partner was. He was a dark-haired, swarthy man with wolfish good looks and he seemed to be keeping Susan well amused.

"Who is that man dancing with Miss Colville, my niece?" she asked Lord Moulton.

"Miss Colville is the beauty?"

"Yes."

"That is Sir Thomas Jeynes."

Dangerfield's rival for the charms of Mrs. Palfrey!

"Is Mrs. Palfrey here?"

"You heard that old scandal? No. Mrs. Palfrey is invited some places but not here, for the Trowbridges are very high sticklers."

At the end of the dance Lord Moulton asked if he might have the honor of the supper dance. Harriet hesitated a little. Perhaps Lord Dangerfield might have forgotten his invitation. But then she said, "No, I regret I cannot. I have already promised that dance to Lord Dangerfield."

He bowed. "Perhaps we shall have another dance? And may I call on you?"

"Gladly," said Harriet. He must be interested in Susan, of course. No sooner had he left than a middle-aged colonel solicited her hand for the next dance. Harriet was gratified but bewildered. With the exception of that supper dance, she had not expected to dance at all.

And then finally the supper dance was announced. For a few dreadful moments she thought the earl had forgotten, but suddenly he was at her side, smiling down at her and saying, "I claim my wager, Miss Tremayne."

After they had performed the cotillion, he led her into the supper room. Susan, Harriet noticed, was being partnered by Charles Courtney. Nothing to worry about there.

"I believe," said Lord Dangerfield, pulling out a chair for her, "that you truly did not expect to be a success yourself."

"Most of my partners have been quite young," said Harriet. "They all want to call, no doubt, to get to know Susan better."

"Can you really underrate yourself so much? Did you not notice that few of your partners solicited Miss Colville for a dance?"

"Yes, but that is because they cannot get near her. I notice you yourself have not managed to secure a dance with her."

"I did not even try," he said, his eyes dancing. "I prefer to admire Griselda from afar."

"When did Griselda, your Griselda, die?"

"What on earth gave you the idea she was dead?"

"When I pointed out to you that you were pining over a dead girl, you did not correct me."

"Ah, that is because she is dead to me."

"But she is not dead?"

"No, she married a worthy squire and has ten children."

"Ten!"

"It is not unusual."

"And has all this childbearing marred her looks?"

"Sadly. She is very fat and quite weatherbeaten."

"Why weatherbeaten?"

"She lives on the Yorkshire moors. Everyone who lives on the Yorkshire moors becomes weather-beaten."

"My lord, I have a sudden feeling that you are lying to me, that this Griselda is a figment of your imagination."

He drew a small miniature out of his pocket. "Cruel Miss Tremayne! There is my Griselda."

Harriet studied the miniature. A beautiful girl, very like Susan, and wearing a blue gown, smiled up at her.

"Why did she turn you down in favor of a mere squire?"

"Alas, I was sent to the wars with my regiment, and when I returned, she was already married."

"And Susan reminds you of her?" asked Harriet nervously.

"To a certain extent. But my Griselda did not have Miss Colville's amazing capacity for chocolates. But enough of my love life. What of yours?"

"Mine? My lord, I am a lady of independent means who has foresworn that side of life."

"That I cannot believe." His gaze fell to the whiteness of her breasts exposed by the low neckline of her gown. "That stylish gown of yours is the envy of every lady, particularly the poor debutantes who are forced to wear white."

"Ah, but it was designed for me by the dressmaker with the help of Lady Dancer."

"But you wear your new clothes with ease. Confess, unbend a little, you are enjoying frivolous society."

Harriet gave a reluctant laugh. "Yes, I am."

"And you will enjoy it even more if you eat something."

They ate in silence for a few moments.

Then Harriet said, "I note that Sir Thomas Jeynes danced with Susan."

"You have been listening to scandal."

"And when we were at Hyde Park toll yesterday, was that . . . ?"

"Miss Tremayne, I would much rather talk about us."

"But what is there to talk about?"

He sighed sentimentally and put his hand on his heart with a theatrical gesture. "We have built up memories, you and I. There is the meal we shared at the inn, the books we read, tea in the garden in Chelsea. Do you not feel us drawing closer together?"

"My lord," said Harriet, her color high, "I am unaccustomed to flirtation, and you are embarrassing me."

"I am not flirting. I tell only the truth, and concentrate on me and stop peering down the table at Miss Colville. She is safe with Courtney."

Susan had eaten a hearty meal and was enjoying a floating island pudding. But her beautiful eyes were fixed on a centerpiece. It was made of toffee, marzipan, and spun sugar. It was King Arthur's castle, complete with the knights of the round table and Queen Guinevere. The candlelight shone on the purity of the sugar. Susan's mouth watered. "When do they serve that?" she said, and it was as well that Harriet's attention was being engaged by Lord Dangerfield, for Susan rudely pointed at the centerpiece with her fork.

Charles Courtney laughed. "I have never known the Trowbridges to serve any of their famous centerpieces. It is my belief that they do not like to ruin it. It is there only for show."

Susan pouted. "I want some."

Charles blushed. He signaled to a footman and whispered, "The young lady wishes some of the centerpiece."

The footman bowed and moved away. Susan gave Charles such a radiant smile that he felt he could die for her. But when the footman returned and murmured that the centerpiece was only for show, Charles felt miserable. "I am afraid that's that," he said to Susan. "I am so sorry."

"*I* think it's silly," said Susan moodily. "It's all made of sweet things, and what's the point of it if it cannot be eaten? Why does she not just have it made of plaster of Paris?"

"I do not know," said Charles miserably, wishing he had the courage to stand up, walk over to the creation, and cut a piece of it. And just a moment before, he had been sure he could die for her, and yet he could not stand up to his hostess over a confection.

Susan took her resentment about King Arthur's castle back to the ballroom. Her hand was claimed for the waltz by Sir Thomas Jeynes. He tried to flirt with her, but those blue eyes only looked vaguely up at him.

"Is something troubling you?" he asked.

"Yes, it is," said Susan forthrightly. "That wonderful King Arthur's castle is *not for eating*! Pooh, it is so ridiculous. I would have loved a piece."

"It is well known that the marchioness likes to display the confectioner's art without serving any. Did you not have enough to eat?"

"No," said Susan bluntly. "I asked nice Mr. Courtney to try to get me a piece, but he could not."

"You should not ask callow youths to help you."

"Meaning you can?" Her eyes sparkled.

"After this dance, instead of joining the promenade, we will repair to the dining room and you may eat your fill."

"And what will the marchioness say?"

"She will not be there."

"Perhaps King Arthur's castle has been removed?"

"I doubt it. Most of the servants leave to have their own supper."

"And you are not afraid of abetting me in such a venture?"

"I am afraid of nothing."

As soon as the last strains of the waltz died away, they walked together to the dining room.

There was no one else there. Sir Thomas gave his wolfish grin and waved an expansive arm toward the castle.

"All yours, dear lady."

He expected it to be a sort of girlish prank. Miss Colville would eat one of the little figures and giggle a bit at her temerity and then they would return to the ballroom before their absence had been remarked on.

But Susan pulled forward a chair and sat down in front of the castle and rubbed her little hands.

She carefully lifted up Sir Lancelot and ate him. "Delicious," she murmured.

Sir Thomas watched amazed as little figure after little figure disappeared into that rosebud mouth. It was when Susan began on the battlements that he became worried. "I think we should return," he said.

Susan paid him not the slightest bit of attention. Sir Thomas strolled to the door of the dining room and looked out. He saw that although sets were forming for a quadrille, Susan's aunt, Miss Tremayne, was saying something to that rat Dangerfield, and they were looking his way. He quickly reentered the ballroom and asked a young lady to dance.

"Where can she be?" Harriet was asking the earl. She turned to Charles Courtney, who was in the same set, and asked, "Have you seen my niece?"

"Not since supper." Charles hesitated and then said in a rush, "I disappointed her dreadfully."

"How so?"

"Miss Colville wished to taste the centerpiece, but it is for show only."

Harriet turned to the earl. "You must forgive me, my lord. I must stop Susan."

"The centerpiece?"

"Yes."

"I will come with you."

They walked together into the dining room.

"You have to admire an appetite like that," declared the earl.

There was very little of the centerpiece left.

Susan was dreamily shoving a little drawbridge into her mouth when Harriet walked up to her.

"Susan! How could you be such a pig? How could you disgrace yourself so thoroughly?"

Susan smiled angelically at them. "It was for eating."

Harriet took out a handkerchief and dipped it into a jug of water, and taking Susan's face firmly by the chin, scrubbed all the sugar crumbs from it.

Then she looked at the earl. "There will be an outcry when this is discovered. What am I to do?"

"Take Miss Colville back to the ballroom immediately. Go along. I will think of something."

Harriet hustled Susan off. The earl looked about him. Then he saw that the fire in the large fireplace at the end of the room was burning low but the embers were hot. He lifted the remains of the centerpiece on its base and thrust the whole thing into the glowing embers. When it had started to burn, he took several logs from the log basket and piled them on top. Better it should have disappeared entirely than be found to have been eaten.

Harriet sat next to Susan and lectured her, ending up with, "And you simply walked in there by yourself and ate the whole thing?"

"No," said Susan sleepily. "That nice Sir Thomas Jeynes took me in."

"Sir Thomas is a *bad man* and you are to have nothing more to do with him. It was a wicked and silly thing to do, and unless Dangerfield can arrange things and if Sir Thomas talks about it, there will be a scandal and you will be damned as greedy. My stars! Debutantes are supposed to eat hardly anything."

Harriet then looked up in surprise, for Lord Moulton was once more asking her to dance, fol-

71

lowed by several men who were obviously hoping for a dance with Susan.

Susan watched her aunt go and then smiled radiantly on her courtiers. "I cannot dance," she said. "I must repair a rip to my gown."

She made her way out of the ballroom and ran lightly down the stairs. The hall was temporarily empty of servants. She pushed open a door and found herself in a rather dark anteroom, the sort of room used for dealing with tradespeople. But it boasted a black horsehair-filled sofa. With a sigh she stretched out on it, put her thumb in her mouth, and fell fast asleep.

And that was where Lord Dangerfield found her after being appealed to by a frantic Harriet.

He shook her awake. "Come along, Miss Colville," he said. "Time to rejoin the dance. Are you trying to frighten your aunt to death?"

"I was so tired," moaned Susan.

"I have no doubt you were, having gorged yourself like a serpent."

"Why do you look at me so angrily?" asked Susan, getting to her feet. "I have never known a gentleman to be angry with me before."

"Perhaps because I am immune to your beauty, miss."

"But not to my aunt's?"

"You think your aunt beautiful?"

"She is not beautiful, but she has become extremely attractive," said Susan, stifling a yawn. "I thought it was the new clothes, but her eyes are very fine, do you not think?"

"Yes, miss, very fine."

"Are you going to marry her?"

"I am weary of the Season before it has begun. I do not think I shall marry anyone."

"Oh, what a pity you do not want Aunt Harriet. But there are plenty of men who do," said Susan.

That artless remark irritated the earl. He thought Harriet was indifferent to him. He had not considered that she might be attracted to someone else, and began to feel angry with her.

The sharp eyes of Sir Thomas Jeynes watched them enter the ballroom together. So that was Dangerfield's interest! His brain began to work busily. He still wanted revenge on Dangerfield because of that old humiliation, and perhaps if he thought hard, he could get at him through Miss Susan Colville.

Harriet dressed very carefully in preparation for calls the following day. Surely Dangerfield would come in person. It was the custom for gentlemen to make calls on the ladies they had danced with the night before. On the other hand, some of them contented themselves with sending a servant with a card.

She tried to put the earl out of her mind. He could not be interested in her. Susan looked the image of his Griselda. Therefore it followed that he meant to get her to favor him so that she would accept his suit when he asked her permission to pay his addresses to her niece.

She went to Susan's bedchamber, where the maid was brushing the girl's hair. "Susan," she said, sitting down next to her, "are you interested in Lord Dangerfield?"

"I am not really interested in anyone, Aunt. I thought Mr. Courtney was pleasant but such a rabbit. I asked him to get me some of that centerpiece and he would not."

"That was not the act of a rabbit, that was the act of a gentleman." Harriet sounded every bit as exasperated as she felt. "Thanks to Lord Dangerfield's quick wits, remnants of the centerpiece were found in the fireplace and the act was blamed on some young bucks who had had too much to drink and fortunately could not remember exactly what they had been doing. Susan, if you get a reputation for being greedy, then no beauty of yours will make you appear attractive. No more chocolates or sweetmeats. The servants have been told not to buy you any. I want your pin money . . . now!"

"But how can I enjoy myself without sugar plums?"

"Very easily. Now, hurry and make ready. Our callers should be arriving soon."

Susan surrendered her pin money. "Dangerfield is already weary of London and has decided not to get married after all," she said. A shadow passed over Harriet's face. Susan felt slightly guilty at having hurt her, for she was sure her aunt was attracted by the earl, but Aunt Harriet deserved to be punished a little for having cut off the supply of sweets, and after all, she had only repeated what the earl himself had said.

So when Lord Dangerfield arrived, it was to find Harriet's drawing room full of gentlemen callers and to be welcomed by a very subdued Harriet, who did not pay him any particular attention. He felt offended. He deserved better than this. Had he not rescued Susan from disgrace? And so he flirted amiably with Susan and stayed only for ten minutes before taking his leave.

Every bit of Harriet's body was aware of his departure. She continued to smile and talk and pour tea. And all the while she thought how she had so recently looked forward to returning to her old life when the Season was over.

After the callers had left, she felt all she wanted to do was lie down with a cologne-soaked towel on her forehead and forget about the earl, the Season, and Susan, but her butler entered and said, "Sir Thomas Jeynes to see you, madam."

"We are not at home."

The butler bowed and left. He returned after a few minutes and said apologetically, "Sir Thomas knows you are at home, madam, and humbly begs a chance to offer his apologies."

Harriet was suddenly too weary to argue. "Send him up."

Sir Thomas entered the drawing room bearing a large bouquet of flowers. He had wondered whether to bring a large box of chocolates for Susan but had decided that after the girl's eating of the centerpiece such a present would not be welcome. He bowed low.

"Miss Tremayne, I am come to offer you my humble apologies for having encouraged your niece in the folly of eating the centerpiece. But she begged so prettily. Do not look daggers at me, ma'am. You surely know how persuasive your niece's beauty can be. Is there anything I can do to make amends?"

"Just do not encourage her in any such prank again," said Harriet.

She sat down. He flipped up the long tails of his coat and sat down opposite her, placing the large bouquet on a side table. "But in faith, madam, you must realize that I expected her to eat only one of

75

the little figures. It was when she started on the battlements that I took fright."

He looked at her in such comical dismay that Harriet began to laugh. "She is a truly dreadful child. Yes, I accept your apology, Sir Thomas."

"That is good. I have another request. Do you go to the opera this evening?"

"Yes, sir, both Miss Colville and myself plan to attend."

"Would you do me the very great honor of allowing me to escort you?"

"You are too kind. But young Mr. Courtney has offered to escort us."

"I see the faint light of old scandal behind your beautiful eyes. You have heard the *on-dit* of my duel with Dangerfield? I thought so. It is old history, Miss Tremayne. You must feel the duties of bringing out an unconventional miss such as Miss Colville onerous. I am a man of the world and could lend you my experience in order to steer the young lady away from unsuitable men."

"Sir, if you are interested in courting Miss Colville yourself . . ."

"Heaven forbid! She is the fairest thing that London has seen this age but too immature for a man of my years." He grinned at her. "Confess, you would dearly like some help."

If she turned up at the opera with Sir Thomas, then perhaps that might annoy Lord Dangerfield, and she did so want to annoy him. Besides, this Sir Thomas was attractive and amusing. What was so very bad about that duel over the mistress, a mistress that she was sure Dangerfield still had in keeping?

She smiled at Sir Thomas. "I am delighted to accept your escort."

He strolled home, feeling well satisfied with himself. The route to Susan's greedy little heart was through Harriet. If he could ruin the girl in some way, then he would get even with Dangerfield.

He had just reached his house when he heard himself being hailed. He turned around.

Verity Palfrey was beckoning to him from a closed carriage. He walked over to her.

"And what can I do for you?" he asked.

"I need your help," she said. "Dangerfield never calls on me. I want to know why."

"And why should I tell you? Why should I not want to see you suffer?"

"Because," said Verity, "you want to make Dangerfield suffer, do you not? And I can help you to do it!"

Chapter Five

Sɪʀ Thomas looked at her curiously. "How can you do it?"

"I swear, if you can get that little simpering miss to lose her heart to you, then he will turn to me."

"That is my part. What is yours?"

"I am invited to the Debenhams' picnic in the Surrey fields tomorrow. I have ascertained that this Susan is invited. You go, too?"

"Yes."

"I shall befriend the young miss."

"Difficult. That dragon who chaperones her, her aunt, will drop a word in her ear."

"Believe me, before that the damage will have been done. Then the field will lie open for you to find the way to her heart."

"I already know the way to Miss Susan's heart."

"That being?"

"Chocolate."

If one has never been in love before, then it is difficult to recognize the beast when it comes along. Such was the state of Harriet's mind. When she had vaguely thought about being in love, she had imagined it a gentle thing, a growing respect and mutual admiration between two people. And so she did not recognize her feelings for Lord Dangerfield as love, this odd mixture of pain and distrust. Not being normally of a jealous nature, she did not recognize, either, in her determination that he was unsuitable for Susan, a desire to have him for herself.

She told Susan that Charles Courtney was to drive them to the picnic, and Susan gave a pink yawn and looked indifferent. Harriet had never attended a fashionable picnic and fondly imagined it would be an informal affair, sitting on the grass and eating simple food.

But Lord and Lady Debenham preferred, like most of the aristocracy, to tame the countryside into a semblance of a comfortable dining room, and so tables were set up on the grass by the river and there were just as many servants to wait upon them as there would have been in the town house, and the fare was sumptuous.

Lord Dangerfield was there, and so, Harriet noticed with a sinking sensation, was his mistress, Verity Palfrey, the lady she had seen at the Hyde Park toll. The day was unusually sultry and hot for early summer. Harriet picked at her food and tried hard not to look at Verity Palfrey. Sir Thomas Jeynes was there as well.

Harriet eyed him speculatively. He had been good company at the opera. She had danced with him at the ball after the performance. But that had not prompted Lord Dangerfield to approach her or even to speak to her. She had hoped he might have been moved to warn her against his one-time rival. He had danced with Susan—twice—and had made her laugh, but when Harriet had asked Susan what he had talked about, what he had said to make her laugh, lazy Susan only looked blank and said she could not remember. She was seated a little away from Harriet beside young Courtney, and they appeared to be getting along famously. What was up with the boy? fretted Harriet. Why couldn't he propose and get the whole nightmare of this Season over with?

She forced herself to talk to her admirer, young Lord Moulton, who was next to her. When the meal ended, people began to rise and walk along by the riverbank.

Verity Palfrey covertly watched Susan, hoping for a chance to speak to the girl alone. And then suddenly she saw her chance. Sir Thomas had approached Harriet and asked her to walk with him; Susan had seen an unfinished chocolate pudding on another table and had promptly forgotten all about Charles and was heading in that direction with a single-minded gleam in her beautiful eyes. Verity moved quickly to her side. "Miss Colville?"

Susan gave her a mildly irritated look, saw over Verity's shoulder a footman take the pudding away, and heaved a little sigh. She focused on Verity.

"I am Mrs. Verity Palfrey," said Verity. "We have not met. You are Miss Colville."

"If we have not been introduced," said Susan vaguely, "then you should not be talking to me."

Verity gave a silvery laugh. "Tish, at an al fresco event like this, one does not stand on ceremony. Walk me a little. I must warn you."

Susan, who was trying to learn to be dutiful, looked around for her aunt, but Harriet was well away from her, walking along on the arm of Sir Thomas Jeynes.

She nodded and walked off with Verity. "What do you want to warn me about?"

"Lord Dangerfield," said Verity.

"The earl? Why? What is up with him?"

"He is a bad man."

Susan frowned. "I think you had best talk to my aunt. He has been all that is kind."

Verity leaned forward. "He is not for you, my little milksop. He is my lover. He has lain in my arms and fondled my breasts."

Susan looked highly irritated. Had this silly woman not accosted her, then she might have been able to get her hands on that pudding. She looked beyond Verity and saw Harriet approaching on the arm of Sir Thomas, and her face cleared.

"Oh, this is all easily dealt with," she said. "Aunt Harriet always knows what to do."

Verity made a desperate clutch at her arm, but Susan tripped up to Harriet and said in her clear, lisping voice, "You must help me, Aunt. There are social situations I still do not know how to handle. That woman there, Verity something, warned me against Lord Dangerfield. She says Lord Dangerfield is her lover and that he has lain in her arms and fondled her breasts."

Harriet felt as if she had been suddenly and violently slapped in the face. The normally urbane Sir Thomas was goggling in horror at Susan.

Harriet was the first to recover. Verity was rapidly making her escape, calling on her maid and footman. "I do not know why such a person has been invited here," she said. "She is a slut, Susan, a member of the fashionable impure. You must not listen to such filth. Do not let her approach you again."

"Very well," said Susan. "But what an odd thing

81

to say. I could have had a chocolate pudding, had she not accosted me."

Harriet saw Lord Dangerfield, and her face set in hard lines. "Excuse me," she said.

At the same time, Susan saw Charles Courtney and would have gone to join him had not Sir Thomas said quickly, "If you want chocolate pudding, Miss Susan, then you shall have it."

"How?" asked Susan, her pretty face betraying the animation it always showed when sweets were mentioned.

"Come with me."

Harriet marched up to the earl. "A word with you."

"Now what have I done?" he asked plaintively.

"Walk a little with me. What I have to say to you, my lord, is not for polite ears."

He took her arm in his. "This is so sudden."

"I do not jest."

They walked away from the other guests and along the edge of the river. The sun was very hot and only a light breeze rustled the young leaves of the willow trees leaning over the water.

Behind them came the jaunty sounds of a military band, hired for the day to entertain the guests. The tune was "The Girl I Left Behind Me," and for a long time afterward Harriet could not listen to that air without a sharp feeling of pain and shame and loss.

He released her arm and turned to face her.

"Now, Miss Tremayne."

"My lord, your mistress, Mrs. Verity Palfrey, accosted Susan and warned her against you."

"The devil she did!"

"There is worse."

"Can there be?"

"She said you had lain with her and . . . and fondled her breasts."

He turned away from her, and his eyes raked the guests.

"I believe she has gone. My lord, Susan has no knowledge, and, I confess, neither have I, of the dark world of the demimondaine. It has been a shocking and disgusting episode. She has achieved her aim, however. I will make sure Susan is never in your company. Pray tell your mistress that if she comes near my niece again, I will tell all London of her behavior, and such invitations as she still can command will be canceled."

"Then listen to *my* advice," he said. "I am not the only sinner in London. There are worse, and one of those is Sir Thomas Jeynes. I believe he has befriended you and your niece in order to spite me."

"You are not only a lecher, but a vain lecher."

"Do not preach to me from the height of your ivory tower, you withered spinster!"

Her hand seemed to move of its own volition. She struck him hard across the face and walked away as fast as she could, longing to escape to the sanctuary of her bedroom and cry her eyes out.

Susan was sitting alone at a table, wolfing down a large chocolate pudding. "Get up!" Harriet spat out. "We are leaving."

Harriet turned and saw Charles Courtney hovering nearby and waved to him. He came hurrying up. "I do not wish to drag you away," said Harriet, her eyes glittering with unshed tears. "Please take us home."

"Gladly," he said. They began to walk toward the

83

carriages. Harriet knew she should stay to thank her hostess, but all she wanted to do was escape. She would send a servant with a note. Lucy, the maid, fussed behind them, itching to tie the bow on the sash on Susan's gown into a better knot. She had been in seventh heaven since her mistress had decided to become fashionable. Not only had she Harriet's new clothes to fuss over, but those of the beautiful Susan.

Charles Courtney drove them home as fast as he could, knowing that there had been a scandal. He refused any offer of refreshment when they reached Berkeley Square, and Harriet thanked him profusely.

"May I call on you tomorrow, at two o'clock, say?" he asked. "I have something of great importance to ask you."

In all her misery, Harriet sensed relief. He was going to propose and she would make sure Susan accepted him.

They were supposed to be going to the opera again that evening, but Harriet told Susan that she wished for a quiet evening at home. She sat down in the privacy of her bedchamber for a good cry. But the tears would not come. Her eyes were dry and sore and there was a lump in her throat. She lay down on the bed and tried to sleep, to run away into sleep, but sleep would not come. A footman scratched at the door and said that Lady Dancer had called.

Harriet answered that she would be with her presently. She rose and splashed cold water on her face and made her way down to the drawing room, feeling tired and old.

Bertha, Lady Dancer, sprang up as Harriet entered the room and cried, "What a scandal! What delicious scandal!"

"What are you talking about?" demanded Harriet.

"Why, the shocking affair at the Debenhams, to be sure. Verity Palfrey has ruined herself completely, but it has had the desired result of bringing young Courtney up to the mark."

Harriet sank down into a chair. "You had better explain."

"Charles Courtney and Mrs. Turnbridge—you know Mrs. Turnbridge, Harriet, fat and forty and ears like a bat. Well, they saw Verity leading Susan aside and then Susan looked startled and headed for you, and so Mrs. Turnbridge followed and heard Susan saying that the Palfrey female had warned her off Dangerfield by telling her she was his mistress and that he had lain with her and *fondled her breasts*. La, that piece of gossip went around like wildfire. Mrs. Palfrey has ruined herself completely. Such language! She will not be invited anywhere now."

"And how did that bring Courtney up to the mark?"

"Mrs. Turnbridge told him, and he said that little Susan ought to have a protector against the wicked world and he would wait no longer. So all's well that ends well. Why, Harriet! You look quite devastated."

Harriet conjured up a wan smile. "You forget. I am not used to the ways of the world. I detest vulgarity and have been subjected to too much of it this day."

Bertha's eyes were shrewd. "A little advice from a friend, Harriet. Such dreadful things happen and

85

one has to accept them with ladylike calm, no matter what. It was going too far to remonstrate with Dangerfield and then slap him in the face publicly. He has great social power."

Harriet turned her head away. "I was overwrought," she said in a stifled voice.

"You should apologize to him."

"He called me a withered spinster."

"Tut! What did you say to provoke such a remark?"

"I said that he was not only a lecher, but a vain lecher."

"Harriet! Fie for shame, fie! Listen to me. Many men have mistresses. Does he frequent the bordellos of Covent Garden? No, not that anyone has heard. He has a mistress of good family and bad morals. All very ordinary and respectable. You are lucky in young Courtney. But any older man, any handsome man, any charming man, is going to have a mistress somewhere. Do you know that Mrs. Turnbridge actually suggested that she thought Dangerfield was interested in *you*?"

"To which you said?"

"To which I replied that no man could look at any other woman while the fair Susan was around. And at least she saw the sense of that. But your worries are over. Do not encourage the attentions of Sir Thomas. I do not trust him."

"He has been all that is kind, Bertha. I prefer to judge people for myself."

"As you will. I will call on you tomorrow to hear the news of Courtney's proposal."

Lord Dangerfield made his way up the stairs to his mistress's drawing room. His heart was heavy.

86

He should never have come to London. Verity had behaved disgracefully, but he had only himself to blame for that. He had been tiring of her for some time and he should have severed the relationship long before this. He felt disgraced and grubby and yet his very guilt made him obscurely blame Harriet for everything. But he should not have insulted her. She would never speak to him again.

Verity was sitting sobbing. He sniffed the air, which was pungent with the smell of onions.

"Onion juice may produce effective tears," he said, "but the smell is awful and it makes your eyes and nose red."

Verity lowered her handkerchief, which she had soaked in onion juice, and glared at him.

"All you achieved this afternoon, Mrs. Palfrey, was to shame yourself and insult me. You will not be surprised to know that our liaison is at an end. You may keep this house, and my lawyers will arrange a generous settlement. I will, however, hold on to the title deeds until the end of the Season. Should you approach either Miss Susan Colville or Miss Harriet Tremayne during that period, you will end up with nothing."

"I was jealous," wailed Verity. "Cannot you understand that?"

"Yes, I can. I will even find it in my heart to forgive you, for you have damaged only yourself. By tomorrow all your social invitations will be canceled."

"I thought we would marry," said Verity.

He was about to shout at her that he would not marry a whore, but bit his lips. She was of good family, he had lain with her, it was a reasonable ambition. He thought ruefully that if he had associated with women of Harriet Tremayne's character earlier, he might have been more alive to the situation. Before Harriet, he had never thought of women as individuals with minds and personality. In other words, he had thought of them in the way that ninety percent of his peers did.

"Let us not have any painful scenes," he said, moving toward the door.

"That little blond minx has bewitched you."

"Believe me, I have no feelings for Miss Colville whatsoever."

He bowed and left. Verity cried then, tears of pure fury. Lord Dangerfield had never got to know her very well. Had he done so, he would have turned about and threatened her with more than the loss of a settlement and a house. For Verity was a passionate woman and a dangerous one. Nothing was ever her fault. Her social disgrace was entirely Susan's doing. She was sure she had not been overheard, therefore it must have been Susan who had told everyone what she had said. Six invitations had already been canceled. Susan must be got rid of . . . permanently.

Lord Dangerfield went to his club. The first person he saw was Charles Courtney, who blushed when he saw him and made to move away.

"No, stay," commanded the earl, and sat down beside him.

"I would like to point out," said Charles rapidly, "that I am about to propose marriage to Miss Susan."

"Excellent idea," said the earl. "My heartfelt congratulations."

"I hope she will have me," said Charles, visibly

relaxing. "I am grateful that you are taking it so well."

"I have no interest in Miss Susan whatsoever," said the earl, wondering how many times he was going to have to point out that fact.

"It is just as well," said Charles, "for her aunt appears to have taken you in extreme dislike. She slapped your face."

"She had good reason to. The provocation was great. I have a great favor to ask of you."

"That being?"

"I have a certain . . . interest . . . in Miss Tremayne."

"Ah-ha!"

"To that end, I would be grateful if you and Miss Colville, without betraying my interest in her, could find ways to put us together."

Charles was flattered that the great Lord Dangerfield should be appealing to him for help. "I will do what I can," he said eagerly, "but why did she slap your face?"

"I called her a withered spinster."

Charles was deeply shocked. "I cannot believe any lady would ever forgive such an insult."

"But you will do your best?"

"Yes, I can but try."

"Then, as Miss Susan has not yet accepted you, may I make a suggestion on how to win her heart?"

"Go on."

"Before you call on her, purchase the finest box of chocolates which Gunter's has on offer. With your hand on your heart, promise her a lifetime of sweetmeats. That will do more for you than talk of love."

"She *is* inordinately fond of sweet things."

"As she does not appear to put on a pound or develop spots, I see no drawback to a happy marriage."

"I am grateful to you and I will indeed do my best to restore your friendship with Miss Tremayne."

Susan accepted with good humor the news that Charles Courtney was to propose to her. "Am I supposed to accept him?" she asked.

"Oh, yes," said Harriet. "He is highly suitable."

"Sir Thomas is quite interesting."

"He has been kind to us, but not a suitable man for you, Susan. Too old and experienced."

"You mean like Dangerfield. Such a pity you are not experienced as well as being old, Aunt Harriet."

"You are impertinent, miss."

"I did not have my morning chocolate. Lucy said you told everyone I was to have tea instead. Without my morning chocolate I feel crotchety."

"I have told you and told you that you will ruin your teeth and your health. Now, go and tell Lucy to make sure you are wearing one of your best gowns."

Harriet waited in the drawing room for Charles. Susan had been told to wait in her room until summoned. The heat was still stifling. The awnings outside covering the windows cast a gloom over the drawing room. Flies buzzed over the gallipots. She felt tired and jaded. All at once she missed her bluestocking friends and longed to return to her old life. Would this Season never end?

Charles Courtney was announced. He came in carrying the largest box of chocolates that Harriet had ever seen. She wanted to protest but then decided that the present would encourage Susan to accept him.

"I am come," he said, "to ask your permission to pay my addresses to Miss Colville."

"You have my permission. Your parents approve?"

"Yes, very much so."

"Then I will send Susan to you. You may have ten minutes alone with her. All that tiresome business of lawyers and settlements can be dealt with later. Although her mother and father trust my judgment, I feel it would be politic for you to go to the country and ask their permission as well. I will give you their direction before you leave. Now I will fetch Susan."

Susan was a vision in white lace and white muslin. Her golden hair shone with health and her big blue eyes were calm and serene—too serene, Harriet thought, for a young lady about to receive a proposal of marriage.

"Am I to see him now?" she asked.

Harriet nodded.

"And what do I say?"

"You say yes," said Harriet tetchily.

"Just yes?"

"You can say you are honored to receive his proposal of marriage."

"And that will make you happy?"

"Oh, Susan, it will. But will it make *you* happy?"

"I suppose it will. I've got to marry someone."

And with those disheartening words, Susan left the room.

She entered the drawing room. Charles promptly held out the large box of chocolates.

Susan's eyes lit up. "How splendid!" She opened the lid and stared greedily down at the contents. She sat on the sofa and balanced the box on her lap, her fingers hovering over the contents.

Charles got down on one knee in front of her.

"Miss Colville?"

"Mmm?" Susan had popped a large chocolate into her mouth and her eyes closed into slits of pleasure.

"Will you do me the very great honor of accepting my hand in marriage?"

"Yes, have a chocolate."

He sat down beside her on the sofa and looked at her ruefully. "Did you really hear what I said?"

"Oh, yes, you offered me marriage and I accepted." Her fingers hovered over the box. He gave an angry little click of annoyance, took the box away from her, and laid it on the sofa on the side away from her. Susan pouted.

"Kiss me, Susan."

"If I kiss you, Charles, may I have another chocolate?"

"Yes," said Charles impatiently, trying to banish a bleak picture of having to entice his wife into the marriage bed by leaving a trail of chocolates leading up to it.

He took her gently in his arms and kissed her soft mouth. Susan sat very still in his embrace, feeling all sorts of new and sweet sensations surging through her. She mumbled something incoherent against his mouth and suddenly wound her arms around his neck and kissed him back, sending them both swimming away into a world of sweetness. At last he raised his mouth from hers and said huskily, "Would you like a chocolate?"

Susan gave him her blinding smile. "More kisses, please," she said.

Harriet, entering the drawing room, stopped short in amazement at the sight of the abandoned couple. She coughed loudly and they broke apart, Charles leaping to his feet, his face flaming. "I—I am so s-sorry," he stammered.

"Think nothing of it," said Harriet, looking at her flushed and happy niece. "Are you engaged to be married?"

"Yes, ma'am."

"Then, as I have things to do, perhaps you might like to take Susan for a drive, and when you return, I will give you her parents' address."

"I can do that," said Susan with a gurgle of laughter. "In fact, I will go with Charles."

"That will not be suitable," said Harriet, "unless I go with you, and I do not wish to make the journey at the moment." She then felt guilty, for there was really nothing to keep her in London. But for some reason she would not admit to herself, she did not want to go.

When a thoroughly besotted Charles Courtney was driving his love toward the park, he suddenly remembered the earl's request.

"My darling," he began.

"Cannot you kiss me again?" demanded Susan impatiently.

"Not in the middle of a busy London street, but we will have plenty of opportunities. I have something to talk to you about concerning your aunt."

"Aunt Harriet?"

"Dangerfield has an interest in her."

"Then he has no hope. She slapped his face."

"Because he called her a withered spinster. Now

he wishes our help in ingratiating himself back into her good graces."

"I should think the damage is irreparable, but we will try. Oh, why, there he is!"

Lord Dangerfield drew his carriage alongside. "I am to marry Charles," said Susan sunnily.

"My felicitations," said the earl.

"And I am out here and Aunt Harriet is at home alone."

"I doubt whether she will receive me."

"Then you may say you are calling on me and she will see you then in order to give you a jaw-me-dead about leaving me alone and to tell you I am betrothed to Charles."

Lord Dangerfield drove off. He could not imagine why he should want so desperately to renew his friendship with such as Harriet Tremayne. But he did know he felt he had behaved disgracefully. He would go. She would see him. And she would accept his humble apology or he would ram it down her throat!

Chapter Six

WHEN HARRIET HEARD that Lord Dangerfield had called, she was about to tell her butler to send him away, but assuming he had really called to see Susan and eager—in Susan's best interests, or so she told herself—to tell the wicked man that Susan was now beyond his reach, she asked the butler to show him up.

When the earl entered, she felt the same little sharp shock she always experienced when she saw him. He was indeed a handsome man with his red hair, powerful build, and clear gray eyes fringed with those thick, sooty lashes. They surveyed each other in silence like two strange cats.

Then Harriet found her voice. "Please sit down, my lord."

He sat down opposite her. She said, "The reason I have granted you an audience . . ."

"An *audience*, Miss Tremayne? Are we become royalty?"

She bit her lip and then went on. "The reason I wanted to see you was to inform you of Susan's engagement to Mr. Charles Courtney."

"I know all about that. I have already offered the happy couple my felicitations."

She surveyed him in surprise. "Then why are you

come? After the insults we traded at the Debenhams, I did not expect to see you again."

"I am sorry I said what I did. Pray accept my
apologies."

"The insult was great."

"So was your calling me a vain lecher."

"Well, I suppose I must accept your apology, and
I offer you mine."

"Thank you." He rose to his feet. "I would be your
friend, Miss Tremayne. London can be a wicked
city. Should you ever need my help, please call on
me."

He bowed and left.

She sat down, feeling bewildered and breathless.
She then became aware her butler was announcing
Sir Thomas Jeynes. She nodded vaguely as a signal
that he was to be admitted.

"I saw Dangerfield leaving," said Sir Thomas. "I
am surprised you saw him."

"He came to apologize," said Harriet.

"Ah-ha! He is trying to get back in your good
graces so as to be near Miss Colville."

"I do not think so. He already knew that Susan
had become engaged to young Courtney."

Sir Thomas went very still, like a lizard on a rock
when a shadow falls on it. "This is news to me," he
said at last.

Harriet walked to the window and looked down
into the street. "I am relieved. Susan is safe. It is
all highly suitable."

A man was selling watercress, another mackerel.
Their salesmen's cries filtered up through the hot,
still air.

"And yet," said Sir Thomas behind her, "I would
still be careful of Dangerfield."

96

She swung around. "Why?"

"Miss Colville is not yet married. I do not believe he will give up that easily."

Despite her own unrealized jealousy, common sense came to Harriet's aid. She said impatiently, "Lord Dangerfield has shown no signs of undying passion for Susan."

"That is not his way. He waits, coiled, like a serpent ready to strike."

"Fiddle."

"We will see. I would be honored if you would accept my escort to the opera tomorrow night."

"Susan and I are going to the Durveys' turtle dinner tonight and I think tomorrow after the Michaelsons' breakfast that we will both enjoy a quiet evening at home."

"But I will see you at the Michaelsons."

"Of course, Sir Thomas."

He bent and kissed her hand. "You are indeed a handsome and intriguing lady, Miss Tremayne."

Harriet smiled at him, his compliment pleasing her inordinately, for although she had said she forgave the earl, his insult still rankled.

The following day was still unusually hot. Lord Dangerfield was not present at the Michaelsons' and Harriet found she had to watch Susan and Charles closely, as the couple had a habit of slipping off together. It was when she finally tracked them for the last time to an arbor in the garden and found them kissing each other, Susan with all the greed that she usually gave to chocolate, that she decided it was time to take Susan home.

She wondered bleakly after she had given the couple a severe reprimand whether she was in fact the withered spinster the earl had accused her of being. She found such "slobbering," as she described it to herself, infinitely distasteful. Everyone knew that passions existed only in the lower class of women. She wondered how Susan had come by such a common streak.

When they returned home to Berkeley Square, Harriet said she would take a bath and suggested that Susan do the same. But Susan had never become used to her aunt's odd desire for baths and went down to the drawing room to write a love letter to Charles.

One of the footmen, John, was bedazzled by Susan, and so when a note had been delivered to him in the street and a guinea handed to him with the request that he deliver it privately to Miss Susan, he had agreed, thinking it a love letter.

Finding her alone in the drawing room, he handed it to her, whispering, "I shouldn't be doing this, miss. Don't tell anyone. I was to give this to you in private."

Intrigued, Susan broke the plain seal and opened the note.

Her eyes widened as she read, "Your betrothed, Mr. Charles Courtney, has a mistress in keeping. If you wish proof of this, tell no one, but come immediately to Plum Lane, off Ludgate Hill, at the sign of the Cock and Bull. A Well-Wisher."

Jealousy was new to Susan, but that was exactly what she felt—raging, blind jealousy. Harriet had returned her pin money to her, so she had more than enough to take a hack. She changed into one of her plainest gowns and bonnets. Then she hung over the banisters, waiting until the hall below was empty of servants, for she knew they had strict instructions that she must never leave the house alone.

She moved slowly and quietly down the stairs, took a quick look around, and let herself out. Berkeley Square was quiet, society resting before the pleasures of the evening. She saw a hack entering the square, hailed it, and asked to be driven to Plum Lane.

Verity Palfrey sat with a complacent smile on her face while her maid dressed her hair for the opera. She was determined to go even though she knew she would be snubbed. She had achieved much that day. When Sir Thomas had come straight to her from Harriet, exclaiming over Susan's engagement, instead of being happy that the girl was no longer any threat, her fury against her mounted. That Susan should ruin her and then go on to become engaged to a young, rich, and eligible man was too much. She appeared to accept the news with languid boredom, but the minute Sir Thomas had left, she went quickly to work. She already had a spy among the servants in Harriet's household, a young maid who arrived after Sir Thomas's visit with the report that Harriet was lying down after bathing. Verity asked the girl if she could pass a note to Susan, but the girl had become terrified and suggested that someone should give the note to John. He took a walk around the square every afternoon.

After she had gone, Verity made her plans. She owned an empty property in Plum Lane. During the years she had squirreled away enough money to buy cheap property when it came on the market.

She summoned her two footmen and told them hurriedly what they must do. She knew both her footmen had prison records and for that reason were prepared to work for her for practically no money at all. Although her late husband had left her a wealthy widow and she had no need, for example, to accept money or property from Lord Dangerfield, she was greedy and always wanted more.

She gave them their instructions and a description of Susan. They were to hire a closed carriage. When the girl appeared at Plum Lane, they were to seize her and hold her inside until dark. Then they were to take her to the center of the Rookeries, that notorious network of slums off Holborn, throw her out of the carriage, and leave her to her fate.

One footman protested. "She'll never come out of there alive or she'll be sold into prostitution."

"Exactly," said Verity. "Now, go about your business."

Harriet was awakened by her agitated maid, Lucy, three hours after she had fallen asleep. "I cannot find Miss Susan anywhere," gasped the maid.

"My dear Lucy, she is probably hiding in some cupboard, sleeping off the effects of that great box of chocolates Mr. Courtney brought her."

"That's the strange thing, ma'am. The box is still in the drawing room, and she has eaten only two of them."

Somehow this little fact began to alarm Harriet. She got out of bed, put on a wrapper, called the servants, and everyone began to search the house.

Susan was nowhere to be found.

John, the footman, felt he would die of sheer guilt. He longed to tell his mistress about that mysterious note but was frightened to do so in case he lost his job. And then, as he searched with the others, he saw the crumpled note lying on the floor behind the writing desk in the drawing room and handed it to Harriet.

Harriet read it with a sinking heart. "How is it that Miss Susan was given this note of hand without anyone informing me?"

But the servants looked at each other in bewilderment, except John, who stared at the floor.

"I must find her," said Harriet. Her thoughts flew to Lord Dangerfield. Not for a moment did she think he had any part in this. All she knew at that moment was that he was tall and strong and had offered his help.

"I will get dressed," she said. "John, you must go to the opera house. You will find Lord Dangerfield there. I hope you find him there. Tell him I need his help."

Glad to do something, John ran off.

Verity Palfrey saw across the opera house the way a footman bent over the earl and how he started to his feet and left his box immediately. Had Harriet summoned him? Verity muttered to her maid, "What is the time?"

The maid took a watch like a turnip out of her reticule. "Nine-thirty, ma'am." Verity gave a catlike smile and settled back in her chair.

Susan alighted from the hack and paid the driver. She was standing staring up at the house, when a man came up behind her. Something hard was shoved in her back. "Do not scream or cry out or I will shoot you," a voice grated in her ear. "Go into the house."

Numb with shock and fear, Susan walked up the worn, shallow steps. The door was opened by another man and she was thrust inside.

"What is happening?" she cried. "Why are you doing this?"

She was pushed into a small, bare room and the door was locked behind her. She heard one man saying to the other, "Now, all we have to do is wait until dark." He raised his voice. "If you scream or cry out, we will kill you."

There was one hard chair in the room. Susan sat down on it and clutched her trembling knees. From outside filtered the roar of the city traffic as carriages plowed up and down Ludgate Hill at the end of Plum Lane. She went to the window and tried it, but it was nailed shut. She thought briefly of hurling the chair against the glass, but the glass might not break, and even if it did, there might not be time to make her escape before they came bursting into the room.

She longed for Charles. But how would he know where she was? And who could have done this to her? And what had they planned for her?

Some almost animal instinct told her she must not cry. She must remain calm and watch and wait for a chance of escape. She said her prayers, thought of Charles, thought of her resolute aunt, and forced herself to be calm.

Shadows lengthened along the room, and then it was dark. The door opened and she saw her captors. One had a gun trained on her and another a candle in a flat stick. They were both tall and had the cold, impassive faces of upper servants. They did not look like thugs or villains.

Susan had taken off her bonnet, and her golden

102

hair gleamed in the candlelight. She stretched out her hands in a gesture of appeal. "Do not harm me," she said.

One man looked at the other and said, "Should we do this? We could turn her loose here and no one would know."

"She'd know somehow," said the other one gruffly. "Let's get it over with. Out, miss."

She, thought Susan bewildered. *She?* Some woman was behind this. Who? Not Harriet. Could it be Aunt Harriet? She had a sudden mad idea that her aunt had become weary of her chocolate eating and laziness and had decided to get rid of her.

She was bundled out into a closed carriage, one man driving, the one with the gun beside her in the carriage. She watched where they were going, down Ludgate Hill and so to Holborn, and then the carriage lurched over the broken cobbles and into the maze of the Rookeries and stopped.

"Out!" commanded the man with the gun.

Her only thought was that she was miraculously still alive. She thought they had been moved by her plight and were allowing her to live. She cast one frightened look at her captor, who had swung open the carriage door, and plunged out. The driver whipped up the horses and the carriage lurched crazily off down the narrow mean street.

Susan stood and looked around her. The rotting houses hung over the street, blocking out any light from the sky. The stench was vile. By the light of a brazier nearby, dark figures stood huddled. She was aware of more figures huddled in doorways. It was like being in a nightmare forest surrounded by wild animals.

And then a woman caught her arm and screeched, "Here's a pretty miss!" Susan wrenched her arm free and started to run. A foot shot out of a doorway and tripped her up and she fell headlong. She twisted around to get up and found she was encircled by people, their faces lit by another brazier, looking like evil faces in hell. The women were grinning, and naked lechery gleamed in the men's eyes. Now Susan knew why she had been left in the Rookeries.

But finding a desperate courage, she struggled to her feet, her golden curls spilling down to her shoulders. In a quiet voice that was more effective than a scream, she said, "Will no one help me?"

Cackling, laughing, grinning, the horrible smelly crowd moved closer, and their dirty, clawlike hands stretched out toward her.

A procession of carriages moved along Plum Lane. In the lead was Harriet with her maid, two burly grooms, and two footmen. Behind her was Lord Dangerfield in his carriage, with his servants, and behind that came Charles Courtney, who had seen Lord Dangerfield hurrying from the opera after being addressed by one of Harriet's servants and had followed him and learned of Harriet's urgent request.

Harriet's two grooms kicked in the door of the house in which Susan had so lately been held prisoner. Harriet rushed in after them, calling, "Susan!"

"Bring lights," shouted Lord Dangerfield. Lanterns were lit. In a small room off the dingy hall they found Susan's bonnet lying on the dusty floorboards.

104

Harriet numbly picked it up. "Where can she be? Who can have done this?"

Lord Dangerfield gathered her to him and held her close. "Stay here. I and my servants and Charles will ask people in the lane if they saw anything."

Harriet sank down in the chair on which Susan had waited and buried her face in her hands.

After what seemed an age, Lord Dangerfield returned, his face stern. One man farther down the lane had told Charles Courtney that he had seen a young girl being taken off in a closed carriage by two men. But where the carriage had gone or what had happened to Susan, no one could tell them.

Jack Barnaby was a burglar and therefore among the aristocracy of the criminal classes. He was strolling through the Rookeries, thinking what a fine, warm night it was and how good it was to be alive. He did not notice the smell or the rags or the bundles of human misery lying in the doorways. He had grown up in the Rookeries and the slums were home to him. He was unusual in that he was tall, almost six feet in height, and broad-shouldered. But only the strong grew past childhood in the Rookeries.

He turned one twisting dark corner and stopped short at the tableau in front of him. By the light of a flaming brazier stood a golden girl, the most beautiful creature he had ever seen. She was surrounded by a crowd of men and women. He walked forward in time to hear her clear voice, "Will no one help me?"

He strode forward and thrust his way to the front of the crowd. "Come with me," he said.

105

Susan stared up at him. He turned around and started to walk away. It flashed through her mind that he was one person as opposed to this terrifying mob, and so she followed him while the crowd fell back, muttering. Jack Barnaby was greatly feared.

He waited on the corner until she came up to him and then continued on his way. Susan stumbled after him along the smelly lanes and alleys. He would probably make her his doxy, she thought miserably, but at least she would be alive.

He stopped at a low doorway and took out a key. "In here," he said.

Susan walked in and followed him up a rickety staircase to a door at the top which he kicked open. The room she entered was relatively well furnished.

"Sit down," he said. Susan took a chair by the empty fireplace, feeling her way through the gloom. He lit a branch of candles, held it up, surveyed her in silence, and slowly shook his head in wonderment.

Then he picked up a squat bottle and held it up. "Gin?"

Susan nodded dumbly. Jack Barnaby was not a savory-looking character. His face was pitted by smallpox, his nose was bent, and his toothless mouth very thin and hard.

He poured her a glass of gin and she tossed it straight back, gasping and spluttering as the fiery liquid worked its way down.

"Why are you here?" he asked, sitting down opposite her and leaning forward and refilling her glass.

"I do not know. I am in the Rookeries, am I not?"

"Yerse, so you've heard o' the Rookeries?"

"Everyone has," said Susan, repressing a shudder.

"So how come you're here?"

"I was abducted, I was taken by two men. I am engaged to a Mr. Charles Courtney. I received a note to say that he had a mistress in keeping, and if I went to an address in Plum Lane, I would find out. So I did. And . . . and two men, one had a gun, forced me inside the house and then, when it was dark, they turned me loose in the Rookeries."

"It's a neat way o' murder," said Jack with something like admiration in his voice.

"Are . . . are you going to murder me?"

"No."

"Are you going to make me your doxy?"

"No, got one."

"So what are you going to do with me?"

Jack surveyed her. He knew she was probably a virgin. He could get a high price for her. But there was something about her beauty and fragility that tugged at a part of his memory. There had been a seamstress once when he was a child who had ended up in the Rookeries under the protection of a brutal man. She had been kind to young Jack. She had had a sweet smile and pretty, fair curls. Her protector had beaten her to death, but she had remained somewhere in Jack's memory as the only person who had ever shown him any kindness.

But the words that came out of his own mouth surprised him. He found himself saying, "Drink up and I'll take you home. But we'll wait until the streets are quiet."

The Bow Street Runners had been called out to search for Susan, and the parish constabulary and the watch.

Harriet sat by the drawing room window while

behind her Lord Dangerfield paced the drawing room. Charles Courtney was crying quietly, but Harriet was beyond crying. She was sick with worry and becoming convinced that she would never see Susan again.

Not once did Lord Dangerfield think that his former mistress might be behind such a plot. He had questioned and questioned Courtney as to who could have known of the engagement so soon, who would wish to stop his marriage. He had visited Sir Thomas Jeynes and threatened him, but the surprise and amazement on that gentleman's face looked all too genuine. Now he was back with Harriet and wishing desperately he could do or say something to alleviate her misery. He glanced at the clock. Two in the morning! He longed to urge Harriet to go to bed but knew she would not follow any such suggestion.

Harriet was obviously hanging on to the hope that if she stayed awake, if she prayed very hard, then somehow Susan would be found safe and well.

And then from outside came the voice of a female raised in drunken song. The night was warm and so all the windows were open.

> "I am a country lass,
> But newly come to Town,
> My cherry's still intact,
> My hair it is worn down."

"I'll silence that vulgar jade," said Lord Dangerfield. He strode through the french windows and out onto the narrow balcony that overlooked the square.

He stared down in amazement. In the flickering

lights of the parish lamps he saw Susan, a tipsy, singing Susan, leaning on the arm of a villainous-looking man.

"It's Susan!" he cried. He ran back through the drawing room and rushed down the stairs with everyone—Harriet, Charles, and the servants—hurtling after him.

Jack saw them coming and took Susan's hand from his arm and gave her a little push forward. Harriet gave a strangled sob and rushed to gather the girl in her arms. Lord Dangerfield set off after Jack, grabbed him by the shoulder, and swung him around. He was about to punch him in the face, when Susan struggled free of Harriet's embrace and shouted, "He saved me. You must not hurt him!"

The earl dropped his fists. "Who are you, fellow?"

"None o' your business, cully." Jack turned again to walk away. And then he heard Susan say the magic words: "Do . . . do not let him go. He musht be rewarded."

He stopped in his tracks.

"I wash taken to the Rookeries," said Susan, swaying in Harriet's embrace, "and would have been murdered had Jack not reshcued me."

Jack surveyed the earl. His eyes fastened on the diamond buried among the snowy folds of the earl's cravat. "That diamond'll do very nice," he said laconically.

The earl pulled out the stick pin and handed the diamond over.

Jack stuck it in his greasy shirt, grinned, winked at Susan, and made his way rapidly out of the square. He guessed the runners were probably looking for the girl, and rescuer or not, they had only to see him to drag him off to the nearest roundhouse.

Susan was tenderly helped indoors and up to the drawing room where, with Charles's arm about her shoulders, she told them of her adventures. "How could you even think I would keep a mistress when I have you?" he exclaimed. Susan gave him a drunken, doting smile and so missed the odd little look the earl flashed in Harriet's direction or the way Harriet suddenly looked at the floor.

"Oh, there'sh shomething elsh," said Susan, looking suddenly weary. "He said *she*."

"Who?" asked Harriet sharply.

"One of my captors. He wash all for letting me go in Plum Lane but the other said *she* would find out." Susan giggled and hiccuped. "For one mad moment, Aunt Harriet, I thought he meant you and you'd become too tired of my lazhiness and chocolate eating." And with that, Susan suddenly closed her eyes, leaned her head against Charles's shoulder, and fell fast asleep.

Harriet stared at the earl and said in a thin voice, "Could this *she* be a Mrs. Verity Palfrey?"

His face looked stern. "I shall go and find out," he said quietly. "I bid you good night."

When Verity was roused by her maid and told that Lord Dangerfield was demanding to see her, she did not fear any recriminations. She could not possibly have been found out. Her agent in the city, who served several other people, had bought the property in Plum Lane recently in his name. This was a precaution Verity took, as she often also bought slum property and was not eager that the ownership should be traced to her. Only her lawyers knew she was the real owner, and they would not talk. And so she merely thought the earl had come to his senses and asked that he be shown upstairs.

The earl strode into the bedroom and stood looking at her as she lay propped up against her lacy pillows. He knew it would be useless to ask her if she had been behind the plot to kill Susan, and so he said, "I am giving you a chance to escape, a chance, madam, you do not deserve."

Verity turned pale. But she said lightly, "Are you foxed? I haven't the faintest idea what you are talking about."

He came and stood over her. "The runners will soon be here. Your minions were recognized. Miss Colville is safe and well, thanks to a miracle. Now, you can lie there and protest your innocence as time passes, time during which you could be leaving the country, never to return. What you had planned for Miss Colville was terrible. You are a monster. If you are here in the morning, I will send the runners to arrest and interrogate your male servants. And they will talk to save their necks. How I ever became involved with scum like you is beyond me."

Verity began to tremble and cry. "I was jealous. Cannot you see that?"

"You fool! Had you been jealous of the girl's aunt, you might have had reason. But to be jealous of a green chit! Get you gone, madam, and never return to this country again."

He turned and strode out. He would need to allay Harriet's fears by telling her the name of the culprit and Harriet, the virgin, would despise him from the bottom of her straitlaced heart for having put her niece in deadly peril through his involvement with a harpy.

Sir Thomas Jeynes was strolling home in the dawn light. He found his steps leading him toward Verity's house. Now that her liaison with Dangerfield was over, perhaps she might be interested in favoring him with some pleasure.

To his surprise, her house was lit from top to bottom and servants were frantically loading up luggage on the roof and in the rumble of a traveling carriage outside.

The street door was standing open. He strolled in and nearly collided with a footman who was struggling under the weight of a large trunk.

"Where is your mistress?" he demanded.

The footman jerked his head in the direction of the upper regions and began to carry the trunk out to the carriage. Sir Thomas ran lightly up the stairs.

He found Verity in traveling clothes, slamming down the lid on another trunk, surrounded by maids.

"What's amiss?" he asked.

"Get out of here!" Verity shouted at the maids. "Don't come back until I call you."

When the maids had scampered from the room, she crashed the door shut behind them and faced him with glittering eyes. "I am leaving the country," she said. "I am ruined."

"What has happened?"

In a flat voice she told him of the plan to get rid of Susan and Dangerfield's threat.

"You fool," he said.

"Fool and double fool," said Verity wearily. "It

was not the chit he was after all the time, but that frump of an aunt."

"You jest."

"No, I had it from his own lips. Oh, Thomas, come with me. I cannot bear to be alone."

He gave her his wolfish smile. "You should have thought of what you were doing before you got rid of me to take up with Dangerfield. Had you told me of your plan, I would have stopped you. There are other ways. But subtlety was never your strong point. Enjoy your exile." He began to laugh, and, still laughing, he made his way out.

But when he reached the end of the street, the smile died on his lips. Harriet Tremayne, by all that was holy! So much easier to get his revenge on Dangerfield through a spinster like Harriet than a glowing girl like Susan who was already betrothed.

Lord Dangerfield had returned to Harriet's in Berkeley Square. He hoped partly that she had gone to bed and so he could put off the moment when he would see the distaste in her eyes, and partly that she would be awake so that he could get the whole sorry business over and done with.

But there were lamps still glowing in the drawing room, and as he approached the house, he saw two runners leaving.

He knocked and was admitted. Miss Tremayne, he learned, was still awake. He went slowly up the stairs to the drawing room, his feet like lead.

Harriet turned around wearily when he was announced. "Oh, it is you, my lord," she said. "I have just informed the runners that Susan is safe and well. There is now the question of this woman ..."

113

"May I be seated?" She nodded. The earl sat down.

He took a deep breath. "Mrs. Palfrey was behind the outrage."

How large her eyes were, he thought.

"Your mistress! Your mistress tried to kill my poor Susan. We must tell the authorities."

"Mrs. Palfrey has been told to leave England and never return. There is no need for scandal. She will not trouble you or Miss Colville again."

"And so she goes free? She should be hanging outside Newgate."

"I agree," he said heavily. "But only think! Were she arrested and brought to trial, there would be the most enormous fuss. Pictures in the print shops, scandal in the newspapers. Endless questioning."

Harriet's face hardened. "I suppose she is gone by now?"

"She will be gone before morning."

"She could be stopped before she reaches the coast."

"I tricked her into a confession. All she has to do is to deny the whole thing. She probably sent two of her servants. She will have rid herself of them already. It would be her word against mine."

"What of the house in Plum Lane? Surely she owns that?"

"Mrs. Palfrey probably does, but she would not have used it if the title were under her name. I assure you, this is the best way, and you no longer have anything to fear from her."

"Indeed! And what if your next mistress is just as villainous?"

"I have no intention of setting up a mistress," he

114

said stiffly. "I can only apologize for having brought danger to you through my association with Mrs. Palfrey. I did not know what she was really like."

"No, I do not suppose you did. In the function she performed, gentlemen do not need to interest themselves in either love or character or tenderness or respect. It depends on wealth and rank, you see. Were you of a lower order and less money, then you could pay a shilling to a trull at the opera house for the same service and with just such indifference to character. But I am very tired, my lord, and cannot sit here for the remainder of the night, berating you over your lack of principles. The matter is finished. Much as I would like to see Mrs. Palfrey dragged to court, I think Susan has suffered enough."

She rose and said with a sort of exhausted dignity, "I am sure you will not be surprised to hear me beg you not to call on us again."

And for once in his privileged life, the earl could think of nothing to say.

He bowed and made for the door. "Stay!" called Harriet. He turned immediately, a faint gleam of hope in his eye.

"You gave your diamond pin to that villain. Send me the bill."

The earl felt he had endured enough. "Don't be silly," he said harshly. He turned on his heel and was gone.

Despite her misery, Harriet slept late the next day. She then went to Susan's bedchamber to find that young lady, sitting at the toilet table and clutching her head.

"I feel like the devil, Aunt Harriet," she moaned. "I shall never touch gin again. You see, Jack said we should wait until the streets were quiet before he took me home and so we drank and drank."

"You will never again drink anything as strong as negus if I have any say in the matter," said Harriet. "Listen, Susan, there is something you must know and must keep to yourself." She told her about Verity Palfrey being behind the abduction.

Susan brightened. "It is all rather romantic, now that I am safe. To have roused such dangerous spite!"

"It is not at all romantic, Susan. But be assured, Dangerfield will not approach us or set foot in this house again."

"Why?"

"Why, you stupid goose? If we had not known him, his mistress would never have become so insanely jealous as to try to take your life. How can you even think of entertaining a man who consorts with a female like that?"

"Because females like that are females like that," said Susan, soaking a handkerchief in cologne and applying it to her forehead. "No female of morals and character is going to embark on such a career when she does not need to. I have heard gossip that Mrs. Palfrey was left a comparatively wealthy widow. And Dangerfield is probably the same age as you are yourself. Would you have him lead the life of a monk? I swear, it is you who are the romantic, Aunt. I listen to gossip at balls and parties and it is not only the gentlemen who have mistresses but the ladies who have lovers. Hardly anyone marries for love. Now, I am lucky with my

116

Charles and I am going back to bed so that I can look pretty for him."

"You always look pretty, Susan. But we shall not be entertaining Dangerfield again."

Chapter Seven

EVERYONE LOVES A lover, or so the saying goes, but by the end of another week Harriet was heartily sick of the billing and cooing of Susan and Charles. Now she really had to act the part of chaperone every time the pair got together. She tried to lecture Susan on the well-known fact that passions of that sort belonged only to the lower orders, to which Susan airily said, "Fiddlesticks! What can you possibly know about it, Aunt?"

She began to long for her old life. Charles had just left for the country, however, to secure Susan's parents' permission, although that had already been given by express post, and Harriet was looking forward to a more tranquil life. With the absence of Charles, Susan became quieter and reluctant to go to many events.

Susan irritated Harriet by saying if Lord Dangerfield was not to be entertained by them, then why was Sir Thomas Jeynes a welcome visitor, he who had also fought a duel over the dreadful Verity. But Sir Thomas had assured Harriet in private that Verity was a dangerous, scheming woman who had entrapped him in her coils. Harriet repeated this to Susan, who raised her delicate eyebrows and said if that excused Sir Thomas, why did it not excuse Lord Dangerfield?

The fact was that although Harriet had said she forgave the earl for having called her a withered spinster, the remark still burned and hurt. Sir Thomas's easy company was like a balm to her wounded soul, and she even turned a deaf ear to her friend Bertha's warnings about him.

Sir Thomas listened so carefully to everything she said, and Harriet was not to know that he was constantly seeking a way to use her to get revenge on Dangerfield.

But the fact was that Sir Thomas was beginning to find Harriet's company a bore. She was an intelligent woman and he did not like intelligent women. When Harriet discussed political matters with him, he found it mildly shocking. The ladies should flatter and coax and tease, cast their eyes down at a compliment and blush prettily, not look you directly in the face and question your judgment on matters that should be strictly masculine preserves. Furthermore, Dangerfield kept clear of her, and surely, if he had any interest in Miss Tremayne, he would have danced with her at least once.

Nor did Harriet seem at all romantically interested in him, Sir Thomas, and even confided to him that she would be glad when the Season was over to return to the quiet company of her bluestocking friends.

"Sounds flat," said Sir Thomas, stifling a yawn. "Do these females go about in society?"

"No, although they are all of good ton," said Harriet. "We meet regularly at Miss Barncastle's house in South Audley Street." She gave a little sigh. "They have not called on me. I hope they have not forgotten about me."

"I am sure they have not," he replied gallantly while idly making a mental note of the name of Miss Barncastle.

A day before Charles was due to return, Harriet woke Susan to remind her that they were to make an early start to go on a barge trip up the Thames, early being eleven o'clock in the morning. But sleepy Susan pleaded, "You go and leave me alone. With that Palfrey woman out of the country, no one can plague me."

Harriet hesitated but then decided that provided she warned the servants to keep a strict guard on Susan to make sure the girl did not leave the house, no harm could surely come to her. She herself was to be escorted by Sir Thomas.

She was almost ready to go, when a note arrived by Sir Thomas's footman to say he was indisposed, Sir Thomas having decided that any revenge on Dangerfield did not lie anymore through Harriet.

The day was fine, the stifling heat and humidity having cleared to be replaced by bright sunlight and a fresh breeze.

She felt suddenly timid at the idea of going by herself, although there would be plenty of people there that she knew. But she stiffened her spine. A barge trip on such a good day would be pleasant.

Her carriage took her to the pier at London Bridge. The first person she saw when she climbed on board was Lord Dangerfield, who was talking to two pretty girls and appeared well entertained.

With relief Harriet then saw Bertha and her husband, Lord Dancer, and went to join them. "Faith, it is good to see you without the dreadful Sir Thomas! But what of Susan?"

"She prefers not to attend," said Harriet. Bertha had been told all about Susan's adventures. "I take great care of her safety."

"I do not think you do," retorted Bertha crossly. "You encourage Sir Thomas, and Mrs. Palfrey was his mistress."

"A long time ago," Harriet pointed out.

"Be on your guard. Dancer, do call the waiter and get us some lemonade."

Lord Dancer smiled amiably and went off to accost a waiter, was waylaid by a party of friends, and promptly forgot about the lemonade.

"Just look at him," said Bertha. "He has forgotten already. My one fear on my wedding day was that he would forget which church we were being married in. Ah, Dangerfield. Be so kind as to supply us with lemonade."

Lord Dangerfield, who had been about to pass them, raised an imperious hand, and a waiter came scurrying up. When the lemonade arrived, Bertha thanked him prettily and then said with a well-manufactured air of surprise, "Why, there is Lady Tasker. I haven't seen her this age!"

She tripped off. Harriet studied her glass of lemonade and Lord Dangerfield studied her bent head. Her face was shielded by a broad-brimmed straw hat. Her gown was of straw-colored silk, and she wore a light flower perfume.

"How is Miss Colville?" asked the earl.

"She is well, but Mr. Courtney is in the country, visiting her parents, and so she does not feel inclined to go out. She has even given up eating chocolates."

People passed and repassed them on the barge. A small orchestra played languid sweet airs in the bows, and the barge slid slowly through the brownish waters of the Thames. As they stood together, they created around them such an air of intensity of feeling that those who were about to approach them backed off.

"Miss Tremayne," said the earl, "before I go away and leave you in peace, I want you to answer me this. Why is it that I am persona non grata because of my past relationship with Mrs. Palfrey and yet Sir Thomas Jeynes is not?"

Harriet had been worrying in the back of her mind about that question ever since Susan had broached it. She could think of no fair reply.

"I was very much shocked by Susan's abduction. I . . . I realize now it must seem odd." She bit her lip. He had come immediately to her help when summoned, he had put his arms around her and comforted her, he had given his diamond pin to that villain.

He stood looking down at her intently. "I am not used to your world, my lord," she said. "One is apt to judge people by their . . . friends."

"And yet I did not judge you by *your* friends."

"What do you mean?"

"The acidulous ladies who glared at you so awfully in Piccadilly."

"That is not the same. Their morals are impeccable."

"Possibly because there has never been any chance and never will be of their morals being under threat."

"That is a dreadful thing to say."

"Sad but true. Look around you, the day is fine,

122

the orchestra is pleasant. Cannot we call a truce?" He held out his hand. "Shall we shake on it?"

She gave him a reluctant smile and then took his hand. He gave her hand a firm shake.

"Now let us talk of more pleasant things. We are bound for Hampton Court. Have you been there before?"

"About eight years ago." Harriet gave a little sigh. She had gone with her friends. It had not been a very enjoyable outing. Miss Barncastle had become lost in the maze, and when they had finally found the guide to direct her out of it, their boat had gone and they had to hire a carriage to take them on the long journey home. Miss Teale and Miss Carrington had called Miss Barncastle a fool and suggested that she and she alone should meet the expense of the carriage. Furthermore, none of them had seen Hampton Court itself, as all the day had been taken up trying to get Miss Barncastle out of the maze. Nor was it the guide's fault. He had been taken up leading a more distinguished party around the royal palace and had warned them not to go into the maze until he was free, but Miss Barncastle had said that she had "a wonderful sense of direction" and had insisted on going in alone.

"I did not have a chance to see Hampton Court itself then," said Harriet aloud.

He took her lemonade glass from her, signaled to a waiter, and exchanged their lemonade for iced champagne. "A toast to renewed friendship, Miss Tremayne," he said, raising his glass.

She was suddenly ridiculously happy. She raised her glass to his. "Friendship," she echoed.

They crossed to the side of the barge. They were

123

moving slowly into the upper reaches of the Thames. The water had changed from brown to blue. The fields and trees on either side, despite the recent heat, were still vivid green.

"So peaceful," said Harriet. "Will the wars never end?"

"We need another Nelson," said the earl. "Although Wellington will possibly do on land what Nelson did on the sea."

"He was a clever and intelligent sailor."

"True. But the French, during the Terror, executed most of their great admirals. You see, as you know, in this country the aristocracy go into the army and the gentry to the navy. In France the aristocracy traditionally became naval officers."

"And yet Napoleon's land armies go from success to success."

"Perhaps," he said dryly, "it is because his marshals lead from the front and our generals from the rear. It is essential to have the command from the front not only because of the morale it gives the troops but someone has to sort out the fog and the mess. By midmorning, with all the gunpowder used, it becomes like fighting in a thick fog and at times one doesn't know foe from friend."

"You were there in the Peninsula?"

"Not only the Peninsula, but India before that."

"Did you sell out?"

"Invalided out."

"What happened?"

"I took a ball in the shoulder and contracted a fever. When I finally recovered after hovering between life and death, it was to learn that my father had died and that I must return to take up my new responsibilities."

"And were the responsibilities heavy? So many of our aristocracy seem to lose fortunes on the card tables that they do not seem to consider their responsibilities at all."

"Such was my late father." The earl looked out across the water, his eyes hooded. "I was still weak and grief-stricken when I arrived home. Because of tutors and then the army, I had not known my parents very well. I remember my mother as a thin, vague lady who kept complaining of feeling ill, and then one day, to everyone's surprise, she actually died of a heart attack. I was five at the time, so I have only a dim memory of her. My father always seemed a bluff, generous man. He would talk a great deal about what a good landlord he was and how his estates were among the finest run in England. My grief over his death did not last very long as I began to plow through the mountain of debts and then found the tenants' farms and cottages in a terrible state of repair. The agent said it was necessary to raise the rents again in order to begin to pay off some of the mountain of debt. I got rid of him."

"Why?"

"If you bleed the tenants dry until they are nigh starving, they have no interest in the land or produce or in anything in the whole world but keeping body and soul together."

"What did you do?"

"I called them all together in the great hall. I told them that no rents would be taken from them for a year. In return, they must work for me as they had never worked before. We would all need to work together. Food would be shared out. I sold my father's jewels and statuary to fund repairs and drainage and phosphates. Those three years were the happiest of my life. And then disaster struck."

"A bad harvest?"

"Worse than that. My great-aunt, who had been a recluse for years, died of smallpox. She left me a very great fortune."

Harriet looked at him in surprise. "But that is not a disaster!"

"Ah, but it was for me, not for my happy tenants. My days had been filled with hard work, with juggling the accounts, with making every penny work, and quite suddenly all the debts were paid and I could afford every improvement, every repair. I set up a school for the children of the tenants, things like that. I thought I would be able to return to the idle life of London, but I confess I have quite often been bored."

He saw a shadow cross her eyes and added quickly, "Not with my present company, I assure you. This is the first time in ages I have officially attended the Season. Before, when I came to London, I indulged in wilder games, trying to persuade myself I deserved a reward."

And part of the reward was Mrs. Palfrey, thought Harriet, but she said aloud, "You appear to have gained a reputation as a heartbreaker. How did you manage that if you did not attend the Season, were absent at the wars, and then on the land for so long?"

"It was based on that stupid duel with Jeynes and then just before that I had an amour with a lady of the ton. I thought it was all very light and frivolous, and then she told me that she would prefer to be married in St. George's in Hanover Square although she knew fashionable weddings were usually now not held in church. I told her that I had no intention of marrying her, had never said anything at all to give her that impression. She tried to commit suicide."

"How dreadful!"

"It was rather dreadful for me, for it was a society suicide, that is, when the lady or gentleman makes sure that there are plenty of attendants to find them when they have taken enough laudanum to make it dramatic rather than fatal. I am well aware, Miss Tremayne, that I am telling you things I have never told anyone before and that such things should not be discussed with a gently bred lady. But there have been enough misunderstandings between us and I do not want any more, and so I would like to tell you about Mrs. Palfrey."

Harriet held up a hand. "Please, don't."

"No," he said firmly. "You must be made to understand. Mrs. Palfrey laughed about the scandal, made it plain that in her eyes our liaison was to be a business arrangement. Her lawyers met with my lawyers and the deal was struck. She was always light and amusing in, yes, I admit it now, often a malicious way. But I began to visit her less and less frequently. I did not think it mattered that much to her. I was unconsciously giving her time to set up a new amour. I never guessed at such depths of rage or jealousy. You must believe me."

"I suppose I must," said Harriet. "But as I have told you, I have been out of the world and until this Season never heard any gossip and so it all seems strange. What will you do now? Set up another mistress?"

"Miss Tremayne! Still, I suppose I deserved that. No, I will not, Miss Tremayne, and you know why."

She looked down at the water. It was very glassy and ripples like those on a Chinese painting ran out from the bows and sent a rolling wash undulating to the bank. She had not the courage to ask him what he meant, did not dare ask him. For if he simply said that his experience with Mrs. Palfrey had put him off women for life, then she knew she would be almost sick with disappointment.

"We have been standing long enough listening to my chatter," he said. He signaled again to a waiter and put their empty glasses on his tray. "We will sit and listen to the orchestra."

And so they sat side by side in amicable silence and listened to Mozart and the plash of the oars and the birdsong from either bank of the river.

At Hampton Court a splendid repast had been laid out for the party on tables on the lawns by the river. Harriet and Lord Dangerfield appeared to neither hear nor see anyone else. Harriet, usually a stickler for good manners, kept forgetting to talk to the gentleman on her other side. She and the earl discussed books and plays, the war, the harvests, the state of the nation, all the subjects a man did not usually talk to a lady about.

Wine was flowing liberally, as was usual at these affairs, and many of the gentlemen and a few of the ladies were becoming very drunk indeed. By the time they all rose to have a tour of the palace, several of the guests were under the table and many of the others were walking unsteadily around the rooms.

All the while, Bertha covertly watched her friend's glowing face and saw the tenderness in Lord

Dangerfield's eyes when he looked at Harriet. So it was Harriet all along, she thought with a burst of proprietary pride. For had not she helped Harriet to choose her modish clothes?

The party next went outside and made for the maze. "Do you particularly want to see it?" Lord Dangerfield asked Harriet.

She shook her head, so he tucked her arm in his and said, "We'll take a gentle promenade in the grounds. Now, isn't that a sad sight?"

Servants were carrying the bodies of the guests who had drunk themselves into unconsciousness back onto the barge. The earl and Harriet moved into the formal gardens, talking easily about the plants and flowers. Harriet confessed that she knew little about gardening, and Lord Dangerfield said that despite his distress at his aunt's legacy, he had benefited from it in that he was able to have the gardens at his home landscaped.

And then they both heard someone ringing a hand bell as a signal that they were to return to the barge. Harriet made to leave, but he held her back. He turned her to him and looked down at her, at that passionate mouth.

"No," she said faintly, but he bent his head and covered her mouth with his own.

The feelings she experienced were devastating. She found she could not hold back and returned his kiss with her whole heart. At last he held her tight and leaned his cheek against hers, feeling her body tremble against his own. The bell sounded once more. He took her arm again. "We do not want to be left behind," he said.

They walked back out of the gardens and down to the river.

On the journey back, they sat side by side again, listening to the orchestra. The air had turned chilly, and Harriet summoned her maid, Lucy, who put a shawl about her shoulders. The folds of the shawl were draped over her hands, and her heart leapt into her mouth when the earl's hand slid under the covering of the stole and clasped her own.

And so hand-clasped, they both sat like people in a trance, unaware that the gossips of London society were studying the pair.

"Look at Dangerfield," said Lord Ampleforth sulkily to a friend. "Smelling of April and May and yet he would do nothing to help me further my suit with Miss Colville and now she is engaged to Courtney."

His friend drawled, "I wonder what Sir Thomas Jeynes will say to this. He's been courting Miss Tremayne."

Lord Ampleforth grinned maliciously. "I'll find out."

"How?"

"I shall have great pleasure in telling him about this romance!"

Harriet said good-bye to Lord Dangerfield at London Bridge. He stood beside her carriage after helping her in and said, "Tomorrow? Come driving with me."

"At what time?"

"Two o'clock."

"Not the fashionable hour?" teased Harriet.

"I am tired of being fashionable."

"Two o'clock, then," said Harriet softly. He stood

back and swept off his hat in a salute as her carriage moved off.

Harriet had no intention of telling Susan about Lord Dangerfield, but she was annoyed to find the girl fast asleep in the middle of her bed, which looked as if a tornado had hit it. Susan lay in a pile of tumbled sheets and blankets, a pretty nightdress ridden up almost to her neck exposing her naked body.

Giving an exclamation of impatience, Harriet tugged the nightgown down. Susan woke up immediately and Harriet saw with contrition the alarmed look in her eyes.

"It is only me, Aunt Harriet," she said.

Susan sat up and looked wildly around. Then she hung over the edge of the bed and peered underneath.

"Susan, Susan! That dreadful woman has gone. No one is here to harm you."

Susan appeared to relax. She stretched and yawned. Harriet noticed that there were shadows under her eyes and her mouth was very red and swollen.

"I am going to call the physician," said Harriet.

"No, no, Aunt. Good heavens. You fuss over me too much." Susan was now completely awake. "I did not tell you for fear of worrying you, but I did not sleep at all well last night because every time my eyes closed, I had nightmares. Did you have a good time?"

"Yes, very pleasant. Susan! What is that bruise on your neck! It looks ugly."

Susan jumped down from the high bed and went over to the mirror and peered at herself. "Oh, that," she said. "I remember. It was in the Rookeries.

131

This dreadful old hag clawed at my neck just before Jack rescued me."

"Never mind, Susan. Charles will be back tomorrow. You both would have enjoyed the barge sail today. The weather was perfect."

"And how goes Sir Thomas?"

"He could not attend. He is indisposed."

"Good."

"Susan!"

"I cannot like him. He looks like a wolf. I keep expecting him to slaver at the jaws."

"That is enough! I am to go driving with Lord Dangerfield at two o'clock tomorrow."

"You are friends again?"

"Yes," said Harriet curtly. "Now, should Mr. Courtney or any other gentleman call while I am out, you are to entertain him or them in the drawing room with Lucy in attendance and the door open."

"Yes, Aunt," said Susan meekly. "I am going to dress and I will join you downstairs and we can have a comfortable coze."

There had been nothing up with Sir Thomas. He had merely not wanted to spend a day with boring Harriet. He was in his club that evening when he found himself being hailed by young Lord Ampleforth.

"Tol rol," said Lord Ampleforth by way of greeting. "You missed the boat today."

"Couldn't be bothered."

"In fact, you missed the boat in more ways than one. Dangerfield and Miss Tremayne are *sooooo* in love."

"Fustian! She does not like to breathe even the same air as he."

"Well, I was there and you weren't and they had eyes only for each other."

Sir Thomas scowled horribly and then demanded, "And what is that to me?"

"Thought you'd like to know," said Ampleforth amiably, and drifted off.

Dammit, thought Sir Thomas savagely. Verity was right all along.

His first idea was to hurry around to Harriet's and drip what poison he could into her ear about the earl. But if she were as enamored with Dangerfield as young Ampleforth thought her to be, then that might serve only to turn her against *him*.

His busy brain rattled through various possibilities, and then he remembered the name Barncastle, Miss Barncastle of South Audley Street. What would that clutch of spinsters think of one of their sisters falling prey to such as Lord Dangerfield? He leaned back in his chair and picked up his glass of wine. Miss Tremayne might not listen to him, but she would listen to *them*.

Lord Dangerfield planned to take Harriet for a quiet drive to the Surrey fields, where he meant to kiss that beautiful mouth again and ask her to marry him. He was later to wonder why he had left the proposal so long, for the day turned out to be a disaster.

The traffic in Piccadilly was very bad. Furthermore, a brewer's dray had overturned, temporarily blocking the street.

Harriet passed the time until they could move on

by telling Lord Dangerfield her worries about Susan. "I found her when I returned yesterday, fast asleep. She said she had been having bad nightmares and the sheets and blankets were all twisted. The poor child had shadows under her eyes and her mouth was very red and swollen. I hope she did not get an infection in the Rookeries. And she had such a bruise on her neck. She said in the Rookeries, some hag attacked her."

"My poor innocent," said the earl.

"What do you mean?"

"I happen to know Courtney was returned yesterday, not today. I may have an evil mind, but if I found a young lady lying in a pile of twisted sheets with shadows under her eyes, swollen lips, and what sounds remarkably like a love bite on her neck, I would assume nightmares were the very last thing she had been having."

"You mean . . . ?" Harriet looked at him aghast.

"I should think so. And there is something else."

"There cannot be!"

"It has been nagging at my mind that Mrs. Palfrey seemed remarkably well informed about your household. One of your servants is not loyal. She must have known exactly when and how to deliver that note. Had you not been asleep, you would have demanded to know the contents, would you not?"

"Oh, this is too much. We must return."

"As you will. But you must allow me some time to turn my carriage in this press."

Although he completed the operation quite quickly, Harriet felt they were taking an age to return to Berkeley Square.

Once there, she hurried before him into the house. The butler in answer to her questions said

134

that Miss Susan had gone to lie down. Mr. Courtney had called but had stayed only ten minutes.

"Did you see him leave?" asked the earl.

"No, my lord, but Miss Susan sent for me and told me that she had sent Lucy out to buy silks, Mr. Courtney had left, and that she was going to her room and did not want to be disturbed.

Her face grim, Harriet mounted the stairs, followed by the earl. "Would you like me to go to her bedchamber?" he asked.

"No, she is my niece and I will deal with her."

They stood together for a moment outside Susan's bedroom door. "Better get it over with," said the earl, and threw open the door.

Charles Courtney and Susan were lying on top of the bed together, arms tightly around each other, mouths devouring each other. They had all their clothes on, which should have relieved Harriet, but she was too shocked at Susan's abandonment to see clearly. She would have run to the bed to pull Susan from it, but the earl drew her back.

"Wait!" he commanded.

He said softly, "Susan is still an innocent and you may say too much while you are so shocked. Leave this to me." He raised his voice and shouted, "Miss Tremayne orders that both of you present yourselves in the drawing room as soon as you have made yourselves respectable."

Harriet allowed him to lead her downstairs. "Now, now," he said gently. "It is not so terrible. They *are* betrothed."

"He was eating her, or that's what it looked like."

"People deeply in love do kiss like that."

Harriet blushed a deep, mortified red. "I have

135

failed as her aunt, as her chaperone. Such behavior is not that of a lady."

"If such behavior were not that of a lady, then the population would decline rapidly and the aristocracy would die out."

"Passions are for the vulgar."

"A stupid idea. Search your own heart, Harriet. Think of the kisses we exchanged at Hampton Court."

Harriet twisted a fold of her skirt in her fingers and looked at the floor. It suddenly occurred to her at that moment, despite the turmoil of her feelings about Susan, that he had kissed her and she had kissed him back, and yet he had said no word of love. *He had not declared his intentions.* He *should* have declared his intentions. He had not. And she had been prepared to go out with him that very day and unescorted by any maid or footman, too. She colored again, unaware that he was watching her with affectionate amusement.

The door opened slowly and Charles and Susan entered hand in hand, looking sheepish.

"Young man," said Lord Dangerfield, "it would be as well if you went this day and got a special license. I am sure Miss Tremayne will agree with me. You may make the explanation to your parents and Miss Colville's parents purely romantic. To put it bluntly, if you do not hurry up, you will be leading a pregnant girl to the altar. No! I know you have kept within reasonable bounds so far, but how long will it last?"

"I am so dreadfully sorry," said Charles.

Susan walked forward. "Pooh! What a fuss about nothing."

"You tricked me, Susan," said Harriet. "Mr.

Courtney, I am sadly disappointed in you. I am shocked. Take yourself off. Until the wedding, which I trust will be as soon as possible—and how I am to explain that to her parents I do not know— you are to behave yourselves."

"Yes, ma'am," mumbled Mr. Courtney.

"I will leave you, too," said Lord Dangerfield, "but I am going only as far as the servants' hall to see if I can find out which one was reporting your movements to Mrs. Palfrey. Do not be too hard on your niece, Miss Tremayne. Such things may shock your sensibilities, but they are very human." He smiled at her, but she turned her face from his.

After an hour's diligent questioning, Dangerfield discovered that a housemaid had left Harriet's employ the day after Susan's abduction, that she had often been absent from work, and that she seemed to have more money than a servant of her class should have. Satisfied at last, he returned upstairs to be told by the butler that Miss Tremayne had gone to lie down and begged to be excused. He told the butler to make sure Miss Tremayne learned the name of the guilty servant and also that she no longer had anything to fear, and took himself off.

Chapter Eight

$\mathcal{A}$T TWO O'CLOCK that same afternoon, Sir Thomas Jeynes called on Miss Barncastle, and when he was ushered in, was delighted to find two other ladies there. He wanted an audience larger than that of Miss Barncastle for what he planned to do.

He was introduced to Miss Teale and Miss Carrington. Having not met Harriet in her dowdy days, he was amazed that such a fashionable lady, although such a prosy one, should have such dull and staid friends. But, he reflected, the duller and plainer, the better.

"We are not acquainted, Sir Thomas," began Miss Barncastle, "but my maid tells me you have urgent news for me concerning a friend."

"Yes, indeed. May I be seated?"

"Pray do. Some wine, or tea, perhaps? The tea is fresh."

Sir Thomas said graciously that he quite doted on tea, although, in fact, he seldom drank anything less heady than wine.

He flipped up his coattails and sat down. It was a dismal room, he thought, glancing quickly around, redolent of good works and good thoughts. The tables were covered in heavy leather-bound tomes. The ladies all had their workbaskets out and had been knitting dingy clothes in the dingy colors ladies always chose when knitting for the poor, as if a bright color might corrupt the lower orders.

He accepted a cup of tea, took a sip, pronounced it delicious, refused a seed cake, and said, "I am come about your friend Miss Tremayne."

Miss Barncastle bridled slightly. In fact, thought Sir Thomas uncharitably, she looked remarkably like a horse.

"Oh, dear," said Miss Teale, all aflutter—an almost pleasurable flutter—"has something *bad* happened?"

"Very bad," said Sir Thomas portentiously, and the ladies shrieked in dismay.

"Have you heard of the Earl of Dangerfield?"

Miss Barncastle said, "We saw Miss Tremayne being driven along Piccadilly by a wickedly handsome man. I overheard someone say that he was the Earl of Dangerfield."

"I need your help, ladies, to save *Miss Tremayne's very soul*."

How they gasped and hovered around him, offering him more tea and cake.

"No, no, I thank you," he begged.

"Is she in peril?" asked Miss Teale, who was a secret reader of the kind of novels the others affected to despise.

"Deadly peril."

"Her life?" cried Miss Carrington.

"Worse than that. Her virtue."

"Alas, I knew only bad would come of poor Harriet venturing into corrupt society," mourned Miss Barncastle, or, rather, her voice mourned while her eyes gleamed with excitement.

"Tell us about poor Harriet," urged Miss Teale.

"Miss Tremayne has fallen in love with Lord Dangerfield. Lord Dangerfield never proposes marriage, only a *carte blanche*."

"Mercy! You must warn her," gasped Miss Carrington.

He stared at the floor and then put a hand to his brow. "Alas, I am not indifferent myself to Miss Tremayne. She might think I was jealous."

Three pinched faces looked back at him, three minds thinking that it was the outside of enough for Harriet Tremayne to have a handsome earl after her without having snared this extremely attractive man as well. But then three minds promptly refused to believe that they had anything other than good thoughts.

"Do not worry," fluted Miss Barncastle. "We will go to dear Harriet directly. She must be *warned*."

Sir Thomas took out a large handkerchief and covered his face as though overcome with emotion. "You are too good," he said in a stifled voice. "Dangerfield is even betting them in the clubs that he can have Miss Tremayne."

When he took his leave after being pressed to "call at any time," he felt he had done a good job. He only hoped he had spiked Dangerfield's guns in time. It would be irritating in the extreme to learn that the man had already proposed.

Harriet was feeling more comfortable. Charles had gone to get a special license. She had sent an express letter to Susan's parents saying they must get ready to travel to London. She said that because of pressing family affairs, Mr. Charles Courtney wished to be married as soon as possible. After

140

worrying for some time about what Charles's parents would think of the rushed wedding, she decided that as Susan was the female catch of the Season, they would probably have no objections at all. That proved to be the case when a letter arrived a few moments later from Mrs. Courtney stating that she would be calling on Harriet the following day to discuss the guest list.

So Harriet was just about to give herself up to the luxury of dreaming of the earl, when she learned that Miss Barncastle, Miss Teale, and Miss Carrington had called. She told the butler to send them in, although she found she really did not want to see them. But she felt guilty at having ignored them for so long.

As soon as she saw their grim, disapproving faces, she knew she had made a mistake.

She forced a smile on her face as three pairs of eyes took in the modishness of her gown and the glossiness of her curls.

"We are come on a serious mission," began Miss Barncastle. "You are encouraging the attentions of Lord Dangerfield."

Harriet's eyes were like ice. "What I do is none of your concern."

"But it is," said Miss Teale. Desire to humble Harriet made her inventive. "My brother, John, is bon ton, as you know, and au fait with what is going on in society. He said that Dangerfield was laying bets in the clubs that he could *have you* outside marriage."

Miss Barncastle and Miss Carrington looked at Miss Teale in admiration, realizing that if one of them had said they knew what was going on in the clubs of London, then Harriet would not have believed them.

"We are so sorry for you, poor misguided thing," cooed Miss Barncastle.

Harriet looked at their sanctimonious faces, and fury, like bile, rose in her throat. She rang the bell. When the butler answered it, she said, "The ladies are leaving. Please escort them out."

"I realize you are upset," said Miss Carrington, "but on calmer reflection you will thank us."

Harriet snapped. *Get out!* she shouted.

When the door was closed behind them, she sat very still, too frightened to move, as if she had just fallen off a tall building. She felt stiff and sore with grief. At last she rose and went to the mirror. In it she saw the old Harriet, dowdy Harriet, spinster Harriet.

How he must have laughed about her with his friends! Her normal good sense had deserted her. Having hitherto shunned the marriage market because she firmly believed she preferred to stay single and independent, she had never realized that she had escaped from life into the dull embraces of ladies of the salon in South Audley Street. She knew only that she had no reason to disbelieve them.

Love can blind people to reality and make the most intelligent stupid. And so Lord Dangerfield, on being told for the second time by Harriet's stone-faced butler that she was "not at home," came to the furious conclusion that Harriet had been playing some game with him, leading him on only to snub him. She was such a frozen spinster, he thought savagely, that her niece and the amorous

Mr. Courtney in bed together must have overset her mind. Harriet's bitter thoughts had also worked against Sir Thomas. She could no longer believe that any man was interested in her, and so he had been refused admittance as well as the earl.

A day before the arrival of Susan's parents, Susan emerged from her dream of love to take in the fact that her aunt was miserable and tetchy. Lucy, the maid, had told her dismally that Miss Tremayne was no longer a credit to her talents as lady's maid, and now wore only the simplest of toilettes and was refusing to see Lord Dangerfield every time he called.

Susan also realized that Harriet was turning down many invitations. She had thought this was because of the flurry of wedding arrangements and pinnings for the wedding gown but, observing her aunt sharply, she noticed that Harriet was indeed looking wretched.

After the dressmaker had been dismissed, Susan sat down on the sofa beside Harriet and took her aunt's hands in a firm grip. "You are looking so blue-deviled," she said. "I thought it was because of all the wedding arrangements, but has it something to do with Dangerfield?"

"That is my affair," said Harriet, withdrawing her hands. "We had best discuss who is to be at the wedding rehearsal . . ."

"No, I won't until you tell me what ails you!"

"If you must. I have made a fool of myself. I thought Lord Dangerfield's intentions were honorable, but he was merely playing a game with me. I have it on good authority that he has been laying bets in the clubs that he can 'have me,' as he so cruelly put it."

"And who was this good authority?"

"My old friends, Miss Carrington, Miss Barncastle, and Miss Teale."

"Those old cats! Good authority! Let me tell you, Aunt, I am now more wise to the ways of the world than you will ever be. Those three frumps are not invited anywhere. How could they possibly know what goes on in the gentlemen's clubs of London? And Charles would have told me if such had been the case. Of course he would. How stupid you are! Did you not think to ask Dangerfield?"

"He would have denied it. And Miss Teale's brother does go about in society, and it was he who told her."

"I do not believe a word of it. Send a note by footman, John, to Dangerfield's and get him here. All that you have to worry about is that he may never forgive you for being such an idiot!"

Harriet covered her face with her hands.

"I cannot bear to see him."

"Then *I* will see him." Susan went to the writing desk and scribbled a note, rang the bell, handed it to John and told him to seek out Lord Dangerfield and bring him back with him immediately.

"But what if it is true?" asked Harriet, white-faced. "What if he laughs at me?"

"Then you will have something genuine to be miserable about instead of moping and mowing over what was nothing more than a fictitious and malicious piece of gossip from three old tabbies! And put another gown on. One of your new ones. You look the veriest frump."

Susan rang the bell again and summoned the maid, Lucy, who brightened on being ordered to make her mistress "like a fashion plate."

Harriet was torn between hope and misery. What if he did not come? What if he *did* come and jeered at her?

When she had just finished being made ready, John put his head around the door to say that Lord Dangerfield was in the drawing room.

Harriet rose and went slowly down the stairs. When she entered the drawing room, Susan, who had been sitting with the earl, rose to her feet and made a hasty exit, slamming the door behind her. Harriet made to open the door so as to observe the conventions, but his harsh voice stopped her. "What is this farrago of nonsense I have been hearing from Miss Colville?"

Harriet hung her head. "My friends, Miss Barncastle, Miss Carrington, and Miss Teale called to inform me that your intentions toward me were dishonorable and that you had been laying bets in the clubs that you could take my virtue."

"And you believed them?"

"Miss Teale said her brother, John, who does frequent the clubs, said so."

His gray eyes filled with contempt. "And so you readily accepted such scurrilous scandal without even asking me whether it was true or not?"

"I thought it must be," said Harriet pleadingly. "I am not young, my lord. I am a spinster beyond the years when most women can accept a proposal of marriage." His eyes softened and he made a move toward her, but her next words stopped him in his tracks. "And ... and you had consorted with such as Mrs. Palfrey—a murderess—or would have been if her plan had succeeded."

"I explained my liaison. I opened my heart to you. But it seems I am never to be forgiven. Well, madam, I do not forgive you for having listened to the spite and malice of your so-called friends!"

He marched from the room.

As he collected his gloves and stick from the butler, he asked for the address of Miss Barncastle, and having secured it, set out in the direction of South Audley Street.

So awesome was his title and presence that Miss Barncastle's maid ushered him in without warning her mistress first.

Miss Barncastle, Miss Teale, and Miss Carrington sat looking up at him, frozen, teacups half raised to their lips.

"So, you are the three witches," he said savagely.

"How dare you burst in here . . . ?" began Miss Barncastle in a thin, reedy voice.

"And how dare you interfere in my life with your scandalous spite?"

"If you mean what we said to dear Harriet," quavered Miss Teale. "We had it on good authority. My own brother . . ."

"So you are Miss Teale, I presume. Well, Miss Teale, I take leave to inform you that I am going in search for your dear brother and I am going to call him out."

"You cannot do that. He is sickly."

"He won't be sickly by the time I have finished with him. He'll be dead."

Miss Teale fell to her knees and held her hands out to him. "Oh, my poor brother. It was not he. It was Sir Thomas Jeynes."

She took one look at the naked rage blazing in the earl's eyes, gave a little hiccup, and fainted dead away.

The other two knelt down beside her and held a hartshorn under her nose and slapped her wrists.

"Tell me one thing," said Lord Dangerfield. "If it was Sir Thomas who poured this silly poison into your ears, then why did you tell Miss Tremayne it was Miss Teale's brother?"

"Neither Miss Carrington nor I did that," said Miss Barncastle. "It was all Miss Teale's idea."

"An idea you were happy to go along with. Why?"

Miss Carrington said, "Sir Thomas told us he was in love with Harriet himself and so she would merely think him jealous."

Without another word, the earl turned and strode from the house.

He tracked Sir Thomas down that evening in White's Club. He was playing cards with a party of dandies. Charles Courtney was there, watching the play, as was Lord Ampleforth.

He drew off his gloves and walked up to the table.

"Jeynes," he said, "you are a cur and a bastard."

Sir Thomas turned pale, but said evenly, "Go away. You are drunk and you are interrupting the game."

"You are not only a cur and a bastard," said the earl, his eyes glittering, "but a whoreson, an insect, a crawling louse."

Silence fell on the gaming room. Everyone sat frozen, some of them wearing silly hats and their coats turned inside out for luck.

Sir Thomas rose to his feet. "You shall pay for those insults."

"By all means." The earl struck him across the face with his gloves. "Name your seconds."

"I'll second you, Jeynes," said Lord Ampleforth gleefully. A Mr. Anderson, a weedy Scot on his first visit to London and delighted that the game had been interrupted, for he had been losing heavily, eagerly volunteered to second Sir Thomas as well.

Charles Courtney said he would act for the earl, as did Lord Tasker.

Lord Dangerfield turned and walked away. The time, place, and weapons would be arranged by the seconds.

Charles found it very difficult to see Susan alone. He longed to tell her about the duel. Sir Thomas wanted swords rather than pistols, and Lord Dangerfield had agreed. The duel was to be fought on Friday morning in Hyde Park at six o'clock.

But Harriet always seemed to be there, a sad Harriet, always watching and listening to make sure the couple was not about to slip off to some convenient bedroom.

But on Wednesday evening, when he escorted both ladies to the opera, he saw his opportunity. Harriet, unlike most of society, became so engrossed in the music that she became deaf and blind to anything else.

As soon as he noticed Harriet leaning forward in the box, her lips slightly parted, he pinched Susan's arm and whispered, "Dangerfield is to fight a duel with Sir Thomas Jeynes."

Susan let out a little shriek, and Harriet immediately turned her head and gave an admonitory "Shhh!"

Both now waited until her attention was once

more focused on the stage. "Why?" asked Susan in a soft voice.

"It was Sir Thomas who told those cats, those friends of Miss Tremayne's, that Lord Dangerfield's intentions were highly dishonorable. He told me this the other day."

"When is this duel?"

"At six o'clock in Hyde Park on Friday morning."

"Does Harriet know?"

"I should not think so."

"Can you stop it?"

Charles looked horrified. "Of course not."

"Is Dangerfield a good swordsman?"

"The best in England."

"And does Sir Thomas know that?"

"I do not think so. The fool prides himself on his swordsmanship and thinks he lost to Dangerfield the last time because it was pistols. It is all very exciting. I have never attended a duel."

Susan sat and worried. She had become very fond of Harriet indeed. There was still hope in her mind that the earl and Harriet might forget their silly differences and make a match of it. Her mother and family, who had been delayed in coming to London because her mother had contracted a mysterious fever, were now on their way. After they arrived, Harriet would have no time for socializing, as they'd have to see to the last-minute arrangements for the wedding. And what use would a dead earl be to Harriet? For perhaps, despite the earl's reputation, Sir Thomas might prove the finer swordsman.

At the opera ball later that evening, Susan sent a smile flashing across the room in the direction of

Sir Thomas. That gentleman promptly secured a dance with her. It was the waltz.

"You are so stupid to fight this duel," said Susan.

He stumbled, apologized, and said, "You should not know of it."

"But I do and I am vastly concerned for you."

"I am well able to give a good account of myself," he said proudly. "I am a fine swordsman."

"But Dangerfield is the best in England."

"I have not heard that!"

"Perhaps because you did not ask. Dangerfield is not the type of man to *brag*."

He fell silent, became abstracted, trod on her toes several times, and Susan hoped she had given him something to worry about. But to make sure, just before the end of the dance she said, "He did not kill you last time, but he means to make a good job of it this time."

Sir Thomas left the ball immediately after his dance with Susan.

He fretted all night about this news of the earl's prowess. In the morning he went to see London's most famous fencing master, Monsieur Duval.

"I am to fight a duel, Monsieur," he said, "and am desirous to perfect my arm."

"Who is it you fight with?" asked the small Frenchman.

"Lord Dangerfield."

"Alas, Sir Thomas, Lord Dangerfield must be the only man who is better than I."

Sir Thomas's heart went right down to his highly polished boots. But he said lightly, "Let us fight. Perhaps it will prove that I am better than you as well."

He fenced well. But each time he was easily defeated.

"If I were you," said Monsieur Duval by way of farewell, "I would draw up my will and make my peace with my Maker."

It was the arrival of her parents that made Susan's mind up for her. Her mother promptly took to her bed and had Harriet running here and there to arrange comforts and physicians for her. The noisy children were here, there, and everywhere. Harriet, Susan decided, would be lost in domesticity, and by the time the wedding was over, the earl might be dead or have killed Sir Thomas and have to flee the country.

So on Thursday night she told a horrified Harriet about the duel.

"I will tell the authorities," wailed Harriet. "This duel must be stopped."

"You cannot do that," said Susan. "No gentleman would forgive you."

"What if he is killed?"

"If he is not killed and yet kills Jeynes, he will need to flee the country," said Susan lugubriously, "and you will never see him again."

Harriet put her hands up to her face in a helpless gesture. "What am I to do?"

Several Colville children erupted into the room and chased one another around and over the furniture, pursued by their harassed governess. Harriet waited until the children had been shooed out. "In order to see him, I would need to go to his home. If I send for him, he may not come."

"Then I will order the carriage for you," said Susan brightly.

"Susan! You know a lady should never visit a gentleman at his home!"

"The circumstances are such that if I were you, I would defy convention. Very well then, go heavily veiled and take a hack."

"What am I to do?" wailed Harriet again.

"I just told you, Aunt. It would be very lily-livered of you to let the poor man go off into death or banishment without seeing him. The duel is over you."

"Over me!"

"Of course. It was Jeynes who told your tiresome friends all those lies about Dangerfield, not dreary Miss Teale's poxy brother. What else was Dangerfield to do? The insult to his reputation was too great."

Harriet made up her mind. "I must go."

"Of course you must," said Susan, "and I will send Lucy to my mother while you dress and find a veil and Mama will keep her so occupied, she will not see you leaving."

The earl was sitting in his library, reading. He planned to retire early and so be fresh for the duel in the morning. Some of his fury had subsided. He had no intention of being forced to flee the country by such as Sir Thomas. Much as he would like to kill him, he decided it would be better to try to wound him severely. Sir Thomas, by some miracle, might, however, prove the better swordsman. His thoughts turned again to Harriet. He was sorry he had left her in such anger and such contempt. He rose and went to a writing desk in the corner. The least he could do was write to her.

His butler entered and said, "There is a lady to see you, my lord."

The earl looked at him coldly. "You should know better."

The butler silently handed him a card turned down at one corner to show that the visitor had called in person rather than sending a servant. The name Miss Harriet Tremayne seemed to leap up at him.

"Show Miss Tremayne in," he said quietly. "Do any of the other servants know she is here?"

"No, my lord."

"Then make sure that they never do. When she is leaving, I will ring for you to make sure there are no servants in the hall."

"Very good, my lord."

Harriet, heavily veiled, was ushered into the library.

She threw back her veil and said pleadingly, "I learned of the duel. I had to see you."

He came forward and took her hands in his. "Do not fear for me. All will be well."

"But if you are killed . . . !"

"I doubt it."

"Then if you kill *him*, you will need to flee the country."

"Much as I would like to, I will endeavor not to." He gave her hands a little tug. "Harriet, Harriet, what is to become of us? Why did you suddenly refuse to see me?"

"You kissed me and yet you did not declare your intentions."

"What a monster you think me, you goose. Of course I want to marry you. I had it all planned so well, you see. We would go to the Surrey fields, and there, far from the fashionable world, and in the sunshine, I would get down on one knee and ask you to be mine. And then the dreadful Susan interfered. I thought your spinster senses had been so shocked by the sight of such naked passion that you had decided to shrink from me."

"No, it was not that, although I was monstrous shocked. Perhaps I have much to learn."

He took her face in his hands. "I will teach you."

Harriet, since that sight of the abandoned Susan, had wondered how any lady could lose her dignity enough to let *that* be done to her. But as his kisses became more searching and the feelings in her body more wanton, it did not seem at all shocking when he removed her bonnet. And then, when his kisses punished her mouth, she did not seem to remember anything about being the independent Miss Tremayne as her body sagged weakly against his. Harriet entered into a red world of passion where nothing mattered, nothing at all.

They kissed and talked and kissed and talked through the night, each going over the first time they had met, the first time they realized they were really in love. And then the earl said softly, "I will call my carriage to take you home."

Harriet sat down in an armchair by the fire. She decided she was not going home. She would stay where she was and try to persuade him to forget about the duel. The fire was warm and she was exhausted with emotion.

The earl returned. Harriet was fast asleep. He hesitated. It was nearly morning, the conventions had already been broken, and they were soon to be married. He fetched a rug and covered her with it and then went upstairs to make himself ready for the duel.

carriage. He leaned across and seized her hand, h
and she was quite limp, as if asleep. He set swiftly for
the road.

Chapter Nine

HARRIET AWOKE SOMETIME later. She stared around the unfamiliar room for a few bewildered moments, and then memory came flooding back.

She remembered him saying he would order a carriage to take her home and then she must have fallen asleep. She looked at the clock. Six! The duel would just be starting.

She jumped up and straightened her clothes, picked up her discarded bonnet and tied it on firmly, blushing as she wondered what the butler would think about her having spent the night in his master's house.

But she managed to escape from the earl's house without any of the servants hearing her. There was no hack in sight, so she set off at a run for Hyde Park. How large and empty it seemed! Where could the duel be taking place? She remembered there was a flat area well beyond the Ring and also remembered having been told that duels were often fought there.

A thin mist was curling around the boles of the trees. Birds were singing and the world seemed young and fresh, but she was assailed by a feeling of doom, that he was dead and that she was too late.

She ran on, holding up her skirts. Her bonnet tumbled off and rolled on the grass, but she did not go back for it. The heavy dew was soaking through her thin slippers. And then at the edge of the field she stopped and let out a great wail of anguish. For Lord Dangerfield was lying in the grass, quite still, his face turned up to the sky. There was no one else in sight, no seconds, no carriages, no Sir Thomas, no surgeon.

She hurtled across the grass, tears streaming down her face, and threw herself down on his chest. Such was her distress, it was a moment before she realized that a pair of strong arms were tightly around her and a voice was saying in her ear, "Steady, Harriet. I'm alive."

Harriet sat up and looked at him in amazement. "You are alive? You are unhurt?"

He sat up as well, gathered her back into his arms, and leaned his chin on top of her curls. "Sir Thomas did not turn up. He has probably run away abroad."

"But *why* . . . why were you lying here?"

"I was so happy I did not have to fight that duel, that I had you, that I was alive, that I sent them all away and lay down and looked at the sky and thought sweet thoughts."

"Your coat is soaking wet!"

"How housewifely you sound, my love. How are you after last night? You are not going to turn against me now that I am safe and well and call me a wicked man for having kissed you all night long?"

"I . . . I cannot believe I behaved with such abandon. Ladies should not . . . do not . . ."

"I will show you how it happens." He tilted her face up. "I kiss you, like this."

157

After a moment, Harriet groaned against his mouth and he rose and pulled her to her feet and said in between kisses, "We are to be . . . married . . . as soon as I . . . get a special . . . license. Let us go home, my home. We are both very tired and should go immediately to bed."

And the hitherto staid Miss Tremayne, who had thought passion was not for ladies, said meekly, "Yes, dear."

Sir Thomas Jeynes had not gone abroad. He had dismissed his servants and was sitting behind closed doors and closed shutters in his town house with nothing other to do than drink and plot revenge. He planned to abduct Harriet, ruin her, and then leave the country.

To that end, he finally ventured out into the street, heavily disguised, to try to seize the opportunity. He saw Harriet, the day after the duel was to have taken place, finally emerge with Susan and get into an open carriage. On horseback, he followed behind. Their carriage finally came to a stop outside Exeter 'Change. Susan and Harriet went inside. Sir Thomas tethered his horse to a post, felt in his pocket for the pistol he had primed before he left home, and followed them inside.

Exeter 'Change was Susan's delight. It was not fashionable but full of all sorts of wonderful bargains, and if looking at the bargains became too tedious, one could always visit the menagerie of wild animals on the upper floor. The reason for the outing was that Harriet was eager to get away from her sister and her noisy children.

Jack Barnaby was strolling about the stalls when he saw Susan and recognized the "flash moll" he had found in the Rookeries. He stood and watched her, again taken aback by her beauty.

Susan was admiring some cherry silk ribbons and Harriet was telling her severely that she did not need any more ribbons, when Harriet suddenly felt a gun pushed into her side and a voice saying, "Do not cry out, Miss Tremayne, or it will be the worse for you. Walk to the door. You, too, Miss Colville." Harriet twisted around and looked up into the face of Sir Thomas Jeynes.

"You!" she said in accents of loathing.

"Pooh!" said Susan. "We are not going anywhere. You can't shoot us in the middle of Exeter 'Change."

"He might, Susan," cried Harriet, ashen-faced.

Jack stared at them both, wondering what had alarmed them. He saw Sir Thomas, saw the way he was pressed close to Harriet, saw Harriet's white face and, at the same time, Susan looked across the stalls and saw him and mouthed, "Help!"

Jack took his cudgel in a stronger grip just as Sir Thomas was saying, "I will shoot you dead, Miss Tremayne, right here. As I have to flee the country anyway, I will be gone before anyone can find me and I will shoot your niece as well."

All in that moment, Harriet felt she had never before had so much to live for. She sent up a prayer for courage and said, "Then shoot us both in cold blood. You will never escape and you will hang at Newgate."

And then, to his horror, Sir Thomas felt a hard object jammed into *his* back and a nasty voice said, "Stand away from the ladies, cully, or I'll shoot a hole in yer rotten back."

"Jack!" cried Susan, giving him a sunny smile.

Sir Thomas turned around and looked into the

evil features of Jack Barnaby. "It was a joke with the ladies, good sir. Only a joke."

A curious crowd was beginning to gather. "We don't want no police," said Jack.

Sir Thomas, seeing Jack was armed with only a cudgel, suddenly darted under the stall with the ribbons, emerged on the other side, and raced for the entrance. "Let him go!" cried Susan.

"Why?" demanded Jack, restrained by her hand on his arm.

"All the fuss and scandal. He will never dare come near us again," said Susan.

"We had best tell Lord Dangerfield," said Harriet. "He will know what to do."

She turned to Jack. "You must come with us. This is the second time you have saved Susan's life. You must be rewarded."

"I want a reward," said Jack slowly. "T'ain't much."

"What is that, sir?"

"A kiss from Miss Susan here."

"Really . . ." Harriet began to protest.

But Susan smiled, stood on tiptoe, and kissed Jack Barnaby full on the mouth. Jack remained for a few moments, stunned, while Harriet led Susan away. Then he shambled out and stood dazed on the pavement while Harriet and Susan climbed into the open carriage. Susan smiled at him wickedly and dropped her lacy handkerchief. He snatched it up and held it at his breast.

They had gone a little distance when Susan said, "Give me your handkerchief, Aunt." Harriet gave her a fine cambric one and Susan began to scrub her mouth. "Faugh! He smelled quite vile. But we were so lucky he was there."

"Dangerfield will know what we must do," said Harriet.

"What is Dangerfield's first name?" asked Susan.

Harriet blushed. "I do not know."

"And you were gone *all night*! Fie for shame, Aunt. Were you ever correct even in his bed? Did you say 'Thank you, my lord. That was very nice.' "

"Susan! You are outrageous!"

Lord Dangerfield heard them out in grim silence. Then he kissed Harriet and said, "Take Susan away, my heart. I will deal with Sir Thomas. I will not be at your wedding, Miss Colville, but I hope you will attend mine. I shall be gone for some days."

"You will be careful," urged Harriet.

"I have you to come back to. I plan to be as fit and well as now. Leave me."

When they had gone, the earl summoned his servants and picked out two footmen and two grooms and told them to go to the gun room and arm themselves. Then they all set out for Sir Thomas's house. The earl looked at it thoughtfully. The shutters were closed and the knocker was off the door, but he had a feeling Sir Thomas was inside.

He turned to his servants. "Break down the door," he ordered. "If the watch comes, I will tell him it is my home and that I have lost the key."

His grooms went around to the mews and came back with a log which they proceeded to use as a battering ram until the door splintered and fell open, hanging crazily on its hinges.

They could not find Sir Thomas until the earl found a locked attic at the top, and in a fit of fury,

161

for he feared Sir Thomas had escaped him, he kicked the door in.

He dodged to the right as Sir Thomas fired at him and then he strode forward and punched him hard on the jaw and Sir Thomas slumped to the floor.

"Carry him out to the carriage," he ordered, "as if he were drunk. Once you have him in the carriage, bind him and gag him."

Ten days later, Sir Thomas, still bound and gagged, was lying in a smelly cabin on board the *Mary Belle*, sailing for America. The captain had orders to free him only when the ship was well out at sea.

The earl sighed with relief. Harriet and London waited for him. He was only sorry he had missed Susan's wedding.

The evening before the wedding day, Harriet, Susan, and Charles were seated in the drawing room. Harriet was relieved that the rehearsal had gone smoothly, although Mrs. Colville had burst into tears, then fainted, and had to be carried out of the church. Susan had been a trifle ripe smelling, not having bathed for some time, but Harriet reflected that the besotted Charles did not seem to mind, and besides, most of London society were smelly anyway.

The butler entered and said, "I beg pardon, ma'am, but there is a villain demanding audience."

Harriet looked amazed. "Then call the watch or send him away."

"He says Miss Susan will be eager to see him. His name is Jack Barnaby."

"This is awkward," said Harriet. "I trust the fool has not fallen in love with you, Susan."

"This Mr. Barnaby," said the butler, "has a woman with him, a slattern."

"He has brought his doxy with him," said Susan with a gurgle of laughter. "Do show them up."

"I wish Dangerfield was here," sighed Harriet. "I fear your villain is about to demand money."

Jack came into the drawing room, dragging a tousled-haired creature behind him. "This here's Maggie," he said, giving her a push forward. Maggie stared about her in awe.

"State your business," said Harriet coldly.

She waited for him to demand money, but his next words surprised her.

"I want to get respekkible," he said.

"Respectable?" echoed Harriet.

"What are we supposed to do?" asked Susan, wide-eyed.

"Well, miss, when we was drinking gin, you told me you was going to get married and your fellah had a tidy property in the country."

"So?"

"So I was thinking that mayhap you had a liddle cottage for me and Maggie to get spliced and bring up kids."

"What kind of work could you do?" asked Charles, finding his voice.

"I'm strong and so's Maggie. Anyfink."

Susan turned to Charles, her eyes shining. "You could find something, could you not?"

"You are right in that I have my own estate," said Charles. "I . . . I . . ."

Susan whispered in his ear. "I will kiss you all over when we are married."

163

Charles turned fiery red and said, "Yes, of course. My direction is Comfrey Hall, near the village of Tupton Magna. Wait, I will give you a note for my steward."

He crossed to the writing desk and began to scribble busily.

Susan sighed. "Is he not a true gentleman?"

Charles finished, sealed the note, and handed it to Jack.

"I am doing this for my betrothed," he said severely. "You must never return to villainy."

Jack nodded in Susan's direction. "We'll serve her till the day we die."

"Very well," said Charles, highly embarrassed, "take yourself off."

When they had gone, Harriet said, "Much as I love you, Susan, I can hardly wait for tomorrow, when you will be Charles's responsibility and not mine."

Susan's wedding was voted a great success. Never had there been a more beautiful bride, vowed society. The crowning success was Mrs. Colville, who cried loudly and noisily throughout, just as a mother ought to do.

Harriet was amused to hear Lady Tasker sigh, "In these wicked days, it is still very moving to see such a beautiful, pure-minded girl going to the altar."

But finally it was all over. Susan had gone off with her husband to Dorset, and the following day Mrs. Colville, who said that the noise of London was sorely affecting her nerves, departed for the country, taking husband and children with her.

And all at once Harriet's life was quiet and ordered again and she thought she might die of boredom.

As the days passed, she began to wonder if she would ever see Lord Dangerfield again. She had found out his first name was Robert and repeated it over and over again. She could not find solace in reading books and spent a great deal of time standing on the balcony overlooking Berkeley Square, hoping all the while to see a tall, red-haired man driving up.

One afternoon she was leaving Hatchard's bookshop in Piccadilly, when she suddenly saw him. He was seated on the box of his traveling carriage with a groom beside him.

Blind to the conventions, she stood on the pavement and shouted, "Robert!" at the top of her voice.

He looked down, saw her, and reined in his horses. She ran up to the carriage. "Get inside," the earl ordered his groom, and reaching down, he held out his hand. Harriet seized it and he lifted her up onto the box beside him.

"Oh, Robert," sighed Harriet. "I was beginning to wonder if I would ever see you again!"

"My darling." He bent his head and kissed her while from behind him a coachman screamed to "Get a move on."

Several passersby began to cheer.

Attracted by the commotion, Miss Barncastle, Miss Carrington, and Miss Teale stopped to stare.

"Harriet is a fallen woman," said Miss Barncastle.

"She can't be a fallen woman," said Miss Teale with a pinched look on her face. "Her forthcoming marriage to Dangerfield has been announced."

"Well," said Miss Barncastle, tossing her head,

"you'd never find me allowing any gentleman to kiss *me* in public."

"As no gentleman is ever likely to kiss you or any of us in public or anywhere else," said Miss Carrington, "you are hardly likely ever to be in the same situation."

It was at least a month before either Miss Barncastle or Miss Teale could bring themselves to speak to Miss Carrington again.

"The wonderful thing," said Miss Harriet Tremayne later, when she was seated on the earl's knees in her own drawing room, "is that because there is no one to chaperone *me*, I can do as I like. Now, tell me what you did with Sir Thomas."

"I and my servants took him to Dover and put him on a ship bound for America. He will be landed in Virginia, where I have good connections. He will find it hard to leave."

"How frightened I was that day in Exeter 'Change," said Harriet. "And yet Susan was so brave. A remarkable young miss."

"She is so enamored of young Courtney, she has even given up gorging herself on sweetmeats, or so you tell me."

"That was until the wedding breakfast. I went abovestairs to help her prepare for her departure, and she was dreamily eating chocolates and some chocolate was melted down the front of her wedding gown."

"People never really change."

"Except that villain Jack. In retrospect, I find it quite moving the way he had decided to reform."

"I hope for the sake of Charles Courtney's silverware that he has." The earl was about to add that

he doubted it very much, but Harriet began to kiss
him and loosen his cravat and so he promptly forgot about everything else.

One bright moonlit night a month later, Jack
Barnaby headed through the park toward Comfrey
Hall. Susan and Charles were entertaining guests
at a dinner party and his "wife," Maggie, he knew,
was on duty in the scullery.

He made his way softly to the kitchen quarters
and looked in the window. Maggie was in the scullery, wearing a print gown and mobcap. She was
scrubbing dishes. He rapped gently on the window
and she looked up and saw him, took a quick look
around, and then jerked her head toward the
kitchen door.

As he reached the door, she opened it and slipped
outside. "Sick o' this life, Jack," she said, taking off
her cap and shaking out her hair.

"Me, too," he growled. "Bin out in the fields all
day."

"I miss the Rookeries, Jack," she whined. "Mrs.
Courtney says all the servants have to learn as
how to read and write. Never had no learning. Why
start now?"

"Come on," said Jack, starting to walk away.

"Where?"

"Lunnon."

She gasped. "Just like that?"

"Got me bag hidden at the outer wall."

She walked after him as she had walked after
him through the Rookeries, several paces behind.

They came to the outer wall, where he picked up
a heavy bag and slung it over his shoulder.

"They was ever so kind to us, Jack," said Maggie. "You didn't steal nuffin' from 'em, did you?"

"As if I would," jeered Jack.

And as he strolled off down the road in the moonlight, the heavy weight of Charles Courtney's best silver candlesticks clinked with a comfortable sound against his back.

THE DREADFUL DEBUTANTE

by Marion Chesney

Mira rides and hunts, trying to please her father and be the son he never had. However, these qualities don't help her during her London Season, where she is an unmitigated disaster. Her wild plan to win the heart of a childhood chum backfires, but this dreadful debutante is on a collision course to love and passion with an unlikely suitor.

Available in your local bookstore.
Published by Fawcett Books.